Luis Algorri
YOU'LL HEAR FROM ME

Luis Algorri, born 1958 in León, is a Spanish writer, musician and journalist. He writes for several newspapers and magazines, including *El País, El Independiente* and *Tiempo*. His first novel *You'll hear from* me was huge success in Spain, France and Germany.

YOU'LL HEAR FROM ME

A NOVEL BY LUIS ALGORRI

TRANSLATED BY DAVID MILLER

BRUNO GMÜNDER

© 2011 Bruno Gmünder Verlag GmbH
Kleiststraße 23–26, 10787 Berlin, Germany
info@brunogmuender.com
Original title: Algún día te escribiré esto
© 1999 Luis Algorri
Translated by David Miller
Cover art: Joris Buiks
Cover photo: © 2005 Howard Roffman, www.howardroffman.com
Printed in South Korea

ISBN 978-3-86787-121-1

More information about Bruno Gmünder books and authors:
www.brunogmuender.com

*I*f I had never seen your face
I would not have suffered so,
yet neither would I have seen your face.
Seeing you has caused such pain,
not seeing you would break my heart.
I would not languish so forlorn,
Yet would have lost much more.

(Spanish madrigal from the Renaissance.)

Part One

*M*uch later on I remembered it was actually him who opened the door to me that afternoon. I had never seen him before. It was Ana's birthday, and there were around ten of us who had noisily climbed up to the fifth floor. There was no elevator. I recall the interminable staircase with its ancient wooden banister, the smell of beeswax and the gray stone steps that had been scrubbed with bleach. Ana and I had only recently met on that day in the country when the two groups—her friends and mine—had joined together for the first time. It had been fun, but above all I'd enjoyed Ana looking at me, whispering into Clara's ear and smiling. Clara's pregnancy was beginning to show, and she was about to get married to Pepo. Shortly afterwards Ana came up to me, extremely nervous, and invited me to her birthday.

I saw him very suddenly when he opened the door to us. It was me who had rung the bell, and his face was now just a couple of feet away from mine. How serious he was. Dark sweater, jeans. Roughly seventeen or eighteen, four or five years younger than me; slim, more or less my height; black hair, long and tousled, almost curly. A shiver ran down my spine. I asked for Ana.

"Have you come for her birthday?"

"Yes."

"They're all in the dining room at the end of the hallway."

We entered. My gift for Ana was a green frog made of wood and attached to a long coil spring; she immediately hung it from the ceiling of her room. Other people gave her books, clothes, CDs

9

and so on. We had a good time. Ana danced with me for most of the evening. She teased me about my clumsiness, taught me how to move my feet, smiled her wonderful smile. We drank quite a lot. I looked for him among the guests, but when I couldn't see him I quickly forgot this rather disagreeable boy who had opened the door to us.

My birthday was two weeks later, and I naturally invited Ana, Clara and the others. We celebrated it with my parents in the countryside. I enjoyed the shimmering poplars, the smell of the river, the campfire, the roast potatoes, and Patxi with his guitar trying to coax us to sing. I smiled when Ana, blushing slightly, suggested we should take a ride along the riverside path on my brother's motorcycle. She put her arms round my waist and I started the engine with a single kick, determined to put her nerves to the test. We rode as fast as we could until the path came to an end. We climbed off, breathing heavily, and I leant the bike against a tree. My legs were shaking.

"Short hair would suit you better. Like a boy."

"You think so?"

"Sure."

"Okay. I've made a date with Clara to go to the hairdresser to-morrow."

All the others had just about finished eating by the time we came back. My father grinned when he saw us, and nudged my mother with his elbow. Our hair was in a mess and our clothes were covered with the fluff that falls from poplars in spring. Ana was wearing my jacket, looking at me with sparkling eyes and not letting go of my arm.

The early days were very intense. Ana placed her arm firmly around my waist whenever we went for a walk. She wore my jacket and I soon reconciled myself to the fact it was no longer mine. Out on the street, or wherever we might be, I likewise soon got used to finding this pretty little head with its freshly cut bob fitting perfectly in the space between my neck and shoulder. We were both keen on the mountains, the songs of Pablo Milanés, van Gogh, her ten month-old niece named Laura, Queen, the writer Julio Cortázar, Mozart, plus the mysterious alchemy and baking expertise that produce a successful *bizcocho de nata*. It didn't take us long to harmonize our respective kissing techniques, and after just a few days a look and a smile were all it took for us to hurriedly search out a dark and secluded doorway. The world beyond had stood still and become irrelevant to us. Everything was going so well.

"Why don't we go up to my place?" asked Ana.

"Are you crazy? What about your parents?" I replied.

"My parents aren't there. They've gone to Salamanca with my grandmother to visit Uncle Ángel. The only person there is my brother, and in any case he's just studying all the time and never comes out of his bedroom."

"Are you sure he doesn't come out?"

"He'd better not. He's still got five exams ahead of him in September."

"But … why do you want us to go to your place?"

Ana smiled. "The frog you gave me is pining for you."

That afternoon at Ana's home was the time we came closest to sleeping together before actually doing so: out of breath, our shoes off, all the buttons on my pants undone, and Ana's blouse lying on the floor. We were startled by a knock at the door.

"What do you want?" shouted Ana.

"Ani?"

"Just wait a moment, goddam—"

The voice in the hallway said something we didn't understand. Ana ran her hands over her face and got up to open the door.

"What on earth do you want?"

"Nothing. Phone for you."

You could hear Ana's bare feet running along the hallway. A very long second passed. The door was ajar. When I recognized him in the semi-darkness of the hallway I felt the blood rushing to my head: the same tousled hair, the same dark sweater, the pallor and the small, hostile eyes. I tried to fasten a wayward button on my jeans.

"Hi, how you doing?" I asked.

"Fine. Hi."

"I think we've met, haven't we? We saw each other briefly at Ana's birthday."

He studied me from head to toe. I decided to leave the button alone.

"Don't know. Sorry, she'll be right back. She's on the phone."

He turned around and disappeared. I heard a door slam somewhere in the apartment. I had just lit a cigarette when Ana came back and closed the door.

"Who is that guy?" I asked.

"José? Well, who do you think? My brother."

"Your brother? But isn't your brother called Eduardo?"

"Yes, but this is a different brother … haven't you met José yet?"

"I think I saw him on your birthday, but I thought he was a friend of yours. There were so many people there …"

"Come on! That's my brother," Ana roared with laughter. "And I've got quite a few more. Surely I told you he has lots of studying to do before September, so that's why he hardly ever leaves the house this summer, although he occasionally goes to the swimming pool. Don't worry, he won't say anything. But tell me—why did you get dressed again so quickly?"

I took her face in both hands and rubbed my nose against hers.

12

"Let me invite you for a mega-pizza; you know where," I suggested.

She laughed again. "With shrimp?"

"With a whole fishing boat full of shrimp!"

"Okay," she smiled, "I'll quickly smarten myself up and then we can go."

We belonged to the same swimming club, and it wasn't long before her parents and mine got to know one another. They didn't sit together to eat, but they said hello and shook hands with the resigned smile of people who know how things stand and that it's best to let nature take its course. Ana and I didn't join them either, but instead spread our towels some distance away from them in the partial shade between the sun and the trees. We lay there until the heat made a swim unavoidable, and the entire process was repeated several times a day. Clara, Pepo, Eduardo and a few others occasionally joined us, but it isn't easy putting up with the cloying sentimentality of a couple who've just fallen in love so they usually left us alone.

It was on one of those days that I was dozing on my towel in the late afternoon sun while Ana lay next to me reading.

"Just look at him! He's already fed up with studying. The boy's got a nerve."

"What?"

"José! He's decided to take the afternoon off. And it's only six weeks till his exams."

I raised my head. "Who?"

"Of course he knows my mother isn't coming today so he immediately takes advantage of it."

"Who on earth are you talking about?"

"José, my brother! Can't you see him there?"

"No, where?"

"With the people on their way to the pool. The one with the blue Speedos."

I felt a chill in my stomach. He was slowly passing us, head bowed and serious as ever, his bare feet carefully picking their way across the grass. His tan made it obvious this wasn't the first time he'd taken the afternoon off. His excessively long arms were typical of a boy who is just emerging from adolescence, almost hairless and without any noticeable muscles beside those that stood out slightly on his chest and upper arms. This slenderness was further accentuated by his Speedos. They were made of navy blue polyester and were similar to those worn by serious swimmers, yet they were slightly too big for him. When viewed from the front, their bagginess together with his negligence in tying the drawstring plus the obvious weight of what was lurking inside made the line of little hairs creeping down from his navel stretch further than usual, thereby hinting at the proximity of his pubic hair. When he turned his back to us the Speedos revealed a firm little ass, moving sinuously yet almost shyly beneath the blue fabric.

"Is something wrong?"

"What?"

"You're sweating and you've gone really pale. Don't you feel well?"

"Me? Never felt better! It's just that it's very hot."

"Come on, put your towel back here in the shade."

"In a second. Let me wake up properly first. I was half asleep, and I was dreaming I was a tortoise in the sun. And us tortoises can only move very, very slowly."

Ana laughed and put our bags a little further into the shade. I finally got up a few minutes later and swiftly wrapped myself in my towel so I wouldn't be obliged to explain the unusual state in which my own swim briefs found themselves.

14

I began to watch out for him. On the afternoons when he showed up at the pool he always did the same thing: he would immediately go to the changing cubicles then emerge wearing his blue Speedos and with a towel slung over his shoulder. He would spend a while in the sun with his friends, then go for a swim and afterwards play a bit of tennis if he could find a partner. He would usually have another swim, enjoy a final spot of sunbathing and then change before leaving, his blue Speedos disappearing every afternoon in a flash of light as he walked up the steps to the changing cubicles. Very occasionally he would greet us by slightly raising his hand, but only if Ana was watching him.

"What exactly does your brother have against me?" I once asked her.

"Against you? Which brother?"

"José."

"You think he's got something against you? But why should that good-for-nothing have something against you if he doesn't know you?"

"That's what I'm saying."

"Forget it, he's just a moron. And quite rude too. And in any case, why should you bother if he's got something against you?"

I had my response at the ready: "Well, surely I need to be getting into your family's good books, don't I?"

Ana roared with laughter and tousled my hair. "What a silly boy you are!"

I didn't like to admit it, but I was starting to sleep badly. I decided to provoke him. One afternoon I saw him sauntering over to the tennis court on his own, carrying a racquet and two tins of balls. He was wearing a white polo shirt. It was barely three o'clock, and the sun was burning like fire in the middle of the sky. He stood on one side of the net and began to practice serves. As soon as there were no balls left he switched sides, gathered them up, and began again. He wasn't that bad. Ana was dozing next to me on her towel.

"I'm just going to hassle your brother for a while," I told her.

"What?"

"I'm going to annoy your disagreeable brother. Wait for me."

"Fine, wake me when you get tired of doing that, which won't be long. He's the most boring boy in the world."

I stood by the fence that surrounded the tennis court so that he had his back to me. I waited until he'd missed three serves in a row.

"You're not moving your wrist properly," I shouted.

He turned around and looked into my eyes. His disdain was once again all too apparent.

"Do you play tennis?"

"I think I could teach you a few things."

He was undecided for a moment. "So have you got your racquet with you?"

My broad grin gave no hint of my evil intentions. "Give me five minutes."

I only needed three. When I returned wearing white shorts and a polo shirt, armed with my racquet, he was still practicing serves. I stood on the other side of the net. It was obvious he felt uncomfortable and was trying to at least show a little friendliness.

"Can you manage a couple of sets?" I asked him.

"If you like we can play a few balls just so you can warm up," he said with a withering smile.

"Don't need to," I replied sarcastically. "And by the way, if that's how you move your wrist I'm more than happy to let you serve."

"Wow, that's very generous!"

He started with two consecutive double faults, but soon overcame his nervousness. The games were long and well balanced. I had the better serve and the better returns, but his volleys were deadly and either through deliberate intent or sheer luck, he placed a humiliating number of balls just an inch inside the line. I had carefully considered my strategy, and laughed brazenly every time he made a mistake until he finally got angry and interrupted the game.

"What exactly are you laughing about all the time?"

"How badly you're playing."

"In actual fact I'm winning right now."

"I'm letting you win, which isn't the same thing."

"You liar! I'm thrashing you. Anyone can see that."

"Oh yeah? You'd better look out then!"

I won three consecutive points on my serve. He won the following game to love and then took the first set. By the time he'd won the second set we were both drenched in sweat. I dropped my racquet, went to the net and held out my hand. He came toward me. It was the very first time I'd seen him smile. He was already handsome, worryingly handsome when he was serious, but his smile was utterly dazzling.

"I owe you an apology," I said. "You've beaten me and you play better than me. Congratulations!"

He shook my hand and smiled. "Hey! You play really well. I was just lucky, and all my shots went in. I don't always get everything in, believe me."

I swallowed. It was obvious he didn't mean what I was thinking.

I leapt over the net, tousled his hair, and placed my hand on his sweat-covered neck. "I think we need a shower, don't we?"

"Sure."

Ana was sitting on her towel, smoking. She looked surprised when she saw the two of us coming toward her. My hand still lay on José's shoulder.

"Your useless brother has just thrashed me in two sets."

"Take no notice of him," murmured José, now frowning again. "He let me win."

"That's not true! He beat me fair and square. But I'll have my revenge, don't worry."

"And where are you going now?" asked Ana.

I waited for him to answer. "We're going for a shower."

Ana sighed and stretched out on the towel again with the look of someone who's convinced that the world is beyond saving if it has so many lunatics in it.

"Okay, okay … And what about you, baby brother? It wouldn't hurt to sit at your desk and study instead of playing tennis, would it?"

"But I'm going straight home afterwards."

"Of course you are. Straight home. As if I didn't know you better, José."

I grabbed him by the shoulder again and dragged him in the direction of the showers. I played the idiot: "So what exactly is it that you have to study?"

"Oh, a whole load of shit. I've got five exams ahead of me in September."

"Which subjects?"

"Well, almost all of them!" he laughed. "History, literature, Latin, physics, God knows what."

"Never!"

"What do you mean?"

"Well, I don't think I'd be much use with physics and 'God knows what', but I could definitely help you with the other three subjects."

"You?"

"Sure. Didn't you realize your sister and I are studying the same things?"

18

"History and art and so on?"

"Exactly."

"Oh. I had no idea." He was blushing slightly. "To be honest, I don't even know your name."

"What? Ana hasn't ever told you my name?"

"No, well yes. I mean, I'm sure you've already noticed we don't get on particularly well."

We were approaching the changing cubicles. I stayed at the bottom of the steps and formally offered him my hand.

"Well then: delighted to meet you, José. I'm Javier."

He couldn't help laughing, and we entered the changing area. Our lockers were almost next to one another. We put the tennis racquets down. He immediately took off his polo shirt and opened the metal locker door with his key. I felt myself shudder.

"And you know something about literature too?"

He took off his shorts and briefs in front of me, without the slightest embarrassment. He was sweating copiously. His ass was just as I had imagined it: firm, small, muscular, without a single hair. His Speedos had left a white area which almost resembled a child's skin and which was in sharp contrast to the honey color of the rest of his body.

"Sure. I've already given lessons myself."

I don't think he realized how nervous I was when I looked at him. His penis, flaccid as it was, didn't appear to be anything special. His pubic hair was as black as the hair on his head. He took a towel and fastened it around his waist.

"Aren't you going to take a shower?"

I felt myself blushing like a child. The spectacle of José in front of me, stark naked, had rooted me to the spot. I stood before him, speechless and still fully dressed, looking at him and trying my best to conceal my nervousness.

"What? Oh, sure. Wait, I'll come with you."

I hesitated for an instant, wondering whether I should undress in front of him or turn my back. *No way,* I thought, *I want to see what kind of face he makes.* Much more slowly than him, I took off my shirt, shorts and briefs. I disingenuously wiped all the sweat off my body with my soaked shirt. I made a point of lingering around my cock, which was neither completely dormant nor completely aroused, and likewise around my balls. *Let's just see whether he notices that there's no comparison,* I said to myself.

"Wow, what a lot of hair you've got … compared to you I'm really just a kid …"

I smiled: "Well, I'd say it's pretty obvious that neither of us are kids."

His facial expression changed abruptly and he blinked nervously.

"What I mean is that kids don't kill themselves playing tennis in August at three o'clock in the afternoon. You'd need to be crazy, wouldn't you?"

He roared with laughter. He was so beautiful when he laughed. I also wrapped a towel around my waist and we proceeded to the showers. He chose the cubicle next to mine and closed the door. I promptly decided I'd suffered enough for one day and began to caress myself. It seemed this was all my cock had been waiting for, and it immediately became as hard as a rock. I couldn't see José, but I could hear the shower splashing next door and could imagine him closing his eyes and straining his face toward the stream of water, soaping his neck, arms and chest barely three feet away from me. Directly behind the tiled wall he was sliding his soapy hand over his perfect buttocks, his little balls and his cock, which thanks to the soap and the rubbing was no longer quite as small and soft as it had been just a moment ago. When the thought struck me that José was perhaps doing just the same as me I couldn't hold out any longer and ejaculated vigorously, my sperm splashing onto the tiles.

"What did you say?" I heard José's voice.

"Eh?"

"Nothing. I just thought you'd said something."

"Me? Nope."

He had heard the groan that had escaped me when I'd come.

"Listen, I'm already finished. I'm going back to the sunbathing area, okay?"

"Wait a second. Let's go together."

I rapidly finished showering and went out of the cubicle, still naked. There he stood, leaning against one of the shower doors, his legs crossed and wearing his blue Speedos. He had lit a cigarette.

"Do you always smoke after you've exhausted yourself playing tennis?"

He laughed: "What about you? Do you always walk around naked after you've showered?"

It was my turn to look very embarrassed; out of sheer nervousness I had left my swim briefs in my locker.

"Hell, you're right! What was I thinking of?"

I would have given ten years of my life for him to know precisely what I'd been thinking of, but that wasn't very likely. I fetched my briefs, pulled them on, and we left the changing room. I already knew precisely what to say: "So, when shall we start?"

"When shall we start what?"

"Hell, José, Latin and history and all that."

"Well, I don't know. I'll have to talk to my parents to see how much they can afford."

I grabbed him firmly by the back of his neck and shook his head. He laughed. His skin was dry by now, and almost unbearably smooth.

I think that was the moment when it all started: when I touched the back of his neck for the first time, pretending I wouldn't stroke

21

it, when my fingers, my hands felt a kind of static electricity on his neck.

"Listen, are you crazy? What kind of nonsense is that? Pay? Would I make my girlfriend's brother pay for private lessons?"

We argued about it for a while. He was clearly embarrassed, and rejected the idea me offering my services free of charge. I didn't let him speak.

"That's enough discussion for now!" I decided. "When do you study?"

"Well, it depends. Usually in the afternoon."

"But you spend your afternoons here!"

"Hey, not all of them."

"Almost all."

"As if! I don't come that often."

I did my best to put on a serious face: "What you need is a bit of discipline. You can spend your mornings devoted to physics and 'God knows what'. From Monday onward I'll come to your house, always between four and six. And afterwards, if you still fancy it, we'll both come to the pool. Okay?"

He looked at me and smiled, his head lowered. "Well, okay."

Suddenly it was him who was laying his hand on the back of my neck, just like I'd previously done to him. I was so surprised that I didn't know how to react. He looked at me and smiled again: that angelic face was finally smiling for me alone, that slender and innocent hand was resting on my skin, and that embarrassed voice was saying: "Hey, thanks. I really mean it."

I laughed and raised my eyebrows.

"Just wait a couple of weeks before you thank me, because I'm a hard taskmaster."

"That's precisely what I need, because I'm really bad."

"We'll see. You'll be a real whizz kid when you take your exams next month. And you'll learn to play tennis too."

We went out. He raised his hand to say goodbye, smiling at me again, then turned around and headed for the sunbathing area. I didn't move. When I saw he'd reached the fence I called after him: "Hey, José!"

He turned toward me.

"I'm not really such a bad person, am I?"

He started to laugh, and shook his head. He waved to me again and disappeared. I saw Ana looking at us, stretched out on her towel. For the first time since I'd gotten to know her I felt angry: not with her, but with myself. I went up to her, smiled, and lay down on the grass.

"Well, how was it?" she enquired.

"Good. He's a really nice guy."

"That just shows you don't know him."

"Well, I'll definitely be getting to know him now. I'm starting private lessons with him on Monday."

"You're giving José lessons?" she asked incredulously.

"Yes. What's so strange about that?"

"Oh, nothing. But he'll ruin your entire summer. He's totally useless. And a lazybones too."

"That's not the impression he gave me. I think he's just a bit absent-minded and needs someone to help him out, that's all."

"You don't know him, believe me."

"Listen, have I already told you that my parents went to Malaga yesterday?"

"Yes. What about it?"

"It means we've got the place to ourselves until the day after tomorrow."

Ana gave me a penetrating stare and took my hand. "Are you being serious?"

"Yes I am. Would you like that?"

"I think so, yes." She paused. "Yes, great!"

I stood up and began to pack our things away.

"What are you doing?"

"I thought we were going now."

Ana looked appalled: "Now? But ... but it's only five o'clock!"

I rubbed my nose against hers: "Hmm, I know," I said softly, "we can easily close the blinds if the light bothers you ..."

It was the first time we made love. I felt happy again.

His long, untidy hair was silhouetted against the light that flooded through the window; that was how he sat every afternoon, his head lowered, engrossed in his books or notes. I would stand next to him and observe in detail the graceful curve of his neck, the profile of his little nose, this self-absorbed face that turned around from time to time and smiled at me. Or we would sit next to each other, my hand resting on his slender shoulder while I talked about irregular verbs, Cervantes or the Thirty Years War. Sometimes a finger would briefly but gently stroke the fabric of his shirt, as if of its own volition, seeming to sense the tenderness of the skin underneath it, so near and yet so unreachable. Sometimes, when he was struggling with a difficult translation, analyzing a sonnet, or had mistaken the date of some obscure battle, my hand was unable to control itself and would plunge into the delicious ocean of his hair, ruffling it without knowing how to extricate itself again, and not wanting to either. I would forget Latin, history, literature, and almost the need to breathe, solely preoccupied by the fear that a sudden impulse might bring my lips closer to his head, his eyes or at least that long, slender neck that disturbed my dreams. This was the beginning of a desperate conflict: I fervently wished that these two hours every afternoon might never end so that I could still have him close, have him to myself, myself alone, yet at the same time I longed for an early release from the exquisite torture

24

of not being able to smother him with kisses, not even embrace him or press his head against my shoulder.

"How am I getting on?" he enquired.

"Do you want to hear the truth?"

"Oh. Am I that bad?"

"No! You're making good progress; or rather *we're* making very good progress. I'm more convinced every day that we'll manage it."

"Trouble is there aren't many days left."

That was correct. The time until the exams was getting shorter and shorter. I couldn't bear the thought that our afternoons together would be a thing of the past, as would the summer and our trips to the open-air pool. He would once again be nothing more than my girlfriend's brother; we'd meet briefly in the hallway and exchange a "hi" and "goodbye" that reflected the silent yet friendly gratitude for the favor I'd done him, although with time this gratitude would likewise dwindle as if nothing had ever happened. But what *was* happening in reality? Nothing. Nothing whatsoever was happening. One guy was merely revising some Latin with another guy for whom those two hours were excruciatingly tedious. Why should it be any different either? Whenever I looked at him during the lesson and this thought came over me I couldn't prevent myself from sitting next to him, grabbing him by the shoulder and pressing him close to me as if he would otherwise fly away at any minute: "Come on, José, you're getting confused! Can't you see it's the accusative?"

Despite his shyness he never objected to me touching him in this way, almost certainly interpreting it as a token of innocent affection or encouragement. It made me come alive. The two hours seemed shorter every time, although I knew that once they were over a fresh source of happiness awaited me: namely the moment when we packed our sports bags and went to the pool.

Ana looked at me in a peculiar way.

"You arrive later every time," she said reproachfully.

"We've only got three weeks left. We have to knuckle down."

"*You've* got three weeks left? I thought it was him who was taking the exams."

"Yes, I know. Don't be pedantic."

"You're taking this thing with José really seriously, aren't you?"

"Nonsense! I like to do things properly."

"But you've been talking about nothing else for the last two weeks. Even Clara has noticed. Every time we go for a drink and start chatting you end up going on about the progress José is making, what José has learnt that afternoon or the previous afternoon, or the day before that, or you talk about the Gallic Wars or Philip II. It gets a bit irritating, Javi. Let's just see if the boy does all right in his exams for once."

Ana wasn't to know that I would have given anything for the exams to be postponed for a week or even two, or for them not to happen at all. I could sense my nerves getting tenser by the day. Every time I saw her, embraced her or kissed her, I had the feeling I was walking blindfold along a narrow path beside a precipice.

On one of these afternoons at the pool, when we had just been swimming, I felt this path crumbling beneath my feet. Ana and I were walking back to our towels, hand in hand, when suddenly she stood still. She nudged me, grinned, and remarked sarcastically:

"Well, just look at that! He seems to have time for all sorts of things."

"Who?"

"Well, who else? The girl doesn't look that bad either, does she?"

I turned around and saw them. José in his blue Speedo was sitting cross-legged on the lawn next to the tennis courts, his arms resting on his thighs. The girl was wearing a black bikini, and was kneeling next to him on the grass. He only had eyes for her. He was talking to her and laughing while he stroked her long dark hair, smiling like I'd never seen him smile before. I felt a tightening in my chest.

"Let's go," I said.

"What's wrong?"

"Nothing. Let's go, please."

"Why are you acting so weird all of a sudden?"

"I'm not acting weird at all. It's just that I'm fed up with this place. We've been coming here all summer like idiots, every afternoon. I can't stand it any longer."

"Well, what can I say? Let's go then. But where do you want to go at seven o'clock in the evening? To the movies? My place?"

"I don't care where we go, only not to your place. C'mon, let's go to the movies."

I've never been able to remember which film we actually saw.

When I entered José's room at four o'clock next day he was already studying.

"Everything okay?"

"Hi Javier, how you doin'?"

"Have you done the translation I gave you yesterday?"

"I've almost finished it."

"Why 'almost'?"

"I didn't have enough time."

I glanced at him. His expression reminded me of a miserable dog that's been thrashed by its master, and he lowered his eyes. I sat at the other end of the table and began to read.

"I believe I've told you hundreds of times that Latin has prepositions that mean different things depending on whether they're combined with the indicative or the subjunctive."

"True. Sorry. You mean this *cum*, don't you?" he asked.

"What else would I mean?"

I carried on reading, or pretending to read, and grit my teeth. The piece of paper was shaking in my hands, and I could barely make out the letters. I don't know how much time passed in this way. I remember suddenly noticing José's voice, soft, almost frightened: "Javier? Are you mad at me?"

I looked deep into his eyes. *Not now*, I told myself.

"Do I have any reason to be mad at you?"

"Don't know …"

"Oh, so you don't know?"

He was unable to hold my gaze. I got up, turned my back to him, folded my arms and stared out of the window into the courtyard.

"You really didn't give me enough time to finish the translation. I kept at it until late last night, but then I also had to do a bit of physics."

"The translation is good. And you know it's good, I don't need to tell you that. Apart from this *cum* with the subjunctive of course."

He stood up in turn, and remained motionless next to the table. I still had my back to him. "What on earth is wrong with you? Have I done something to you?"

I breathed in deeply through my nose

"What's wrong with me? Shall I tell you what's wrong with me?"

I didn't wait for an answer.

"What's wrong with me is that I care about your exams a great deal more than you do. What's wrong with me is that I spend hours preparing our sessions here, searching for books, notes, all sorts of things, just to make everything as easy and pleasant as possible. What's wrong with me is that we only have nine days until your history exam and I'm feeling really anxious, whereas you have the time and the energy to make out with a girl nine days before your

28

exam, José! You have the nerve to be making out with a dumb fifteen year-old girl at the very moment when you ought to be shut up in here like a monk in a monastery! And that's what I've been working my ass off for! You wanted to know what's wrong with me? Well fine, now you know: that's what's wrong with me."

I immediately felt like a total jerk. I was lying to him and I knew it. A leaden silence filled the room. I had an almost unbearable desire to leave, but I could feel José's eyes on the back of my neck, and that made me pause.

"I wasn't making out with Beatriz," he murmured. I noticed that his voice sounded rather fragile. I answered without turning around.

"I saw you. We saw you, Ana and me. Yesterday at the pool."

"Javier, I wasn't making out with Beatriz, honestly! She was only introduced to me yesterday afternoon. I spent a quarter of an hour with her and the others, and after that I came straight home. You can't … you can't be implying that …"

I said nothing. Two doves in the courtyard were at that moment engaged in a most vigorous flirtation. The male, his feathers fluffed up and head lowered, was repeatedly encircling the female who was pretending not to notice. I trembled like a leaf when I felt José timidly placing his hand on my shoulder.

"Javier …"

I turned around, and all the blood within my body rushed to my stomach. My God, he was crying. José was crying like a little boy. Tears were rolling down his cheeks while his black eyes looked at me, full of anguish.

"You can't … I haven't … I …"

And then he hugged me. To be precise, he threw himself against me and then slumped, as if in a faint. I thought I would die of happiness.

He buried his face into my neck, put his arms around me and

began to sob. Then he got hiccoughs and his whole body shook. I couldn't stand it any longer. I took him by his narrow waist and hugged him as I had never hugged anyone before. I spent what seemed like an eternity stroking his head, neck and shoulders. I couldn't prevent my lips from touching his hair, his ear, and the bottom of his cheek. He was still crying, completely drained.

"Come on, José, calm down."

"You can't say that I … you can't be mad at me …"

"I'm not mad at you, José. What are you talking about?"

He removed his head from my shoulder and took my face in both hands, looking steadily and intensely into my eyes through this flood of tears. His mouth was six inches away from mine. He gasped for breath several times as he tried to calm himself.

"I can't bear it when you're mad at me."

I closed my eyelids tight shut, but was now unable to stop my own tears from flowing. I hugged him even tighter, removing my face from his hands and caressing his cheek with mine.

"Don't say that, José."

"But it's the truth, I swear it's the truth. You don't know what you're doing for me, what you mean to me, how I feel when I'm with you …"

He started to cry again, and pressed his head against my shoulder. We remained like that, locked in a firm embrace and both of us crying; for all I cared it could have gone on forever. *Now say it*, I thought. I wished with all my strength: *tell me you love me, you idiot, say it and kiss me until I suffocate.*

But he didn't. He contented himself with sobbing, ever more softly, occasionally gasping for breath and trying to calm himself down. I decided I had resisted temptation for long enough. I wanted to make a joke to mollify him, to tell him we ought to be working and that it would be better to finish the translation, but my lips wouldn't obey me.

"It's the other way round: *you* don't know what you're doing for me," I heard myself say.

I was entranced by the sheer innocence of his gaze, his messed-up hair, this puffy, tear-stained face upon which a delicate smile was slowly beginning to form, the most beautiful smile the world had ever seen. I began to tremble with a joy so intense that it almost seemed like fear. It was then that the idea came to me like a flash of lightning.

"You told me a little while ago that you like the mountains."

"Yes."

"Do you know the Picos de Europa?"

"A little. I think I was there with my parents once when I was very small."

I began to tidy the hair away from his forehead "If you pass all five exams I'll invite you to spend five days camping with me in the Valdeón valley. One day for every exam you pass. Just the two of us."

"Do you really mean that?" He batted his eyelids, looking like a small child about to be given his Christmas presents.

"I promise."

"But I haven't got a tent."

"I've got one."

"But I haven't got any money, and my parents ..."

"I told you. It's my treat."

"But my rucksack is broken."

"You can have one of mine. What's wrong? Any more objections? If you don't want to ..."

"Of course I do!" he exclaimed, hugging me again with all his might. "It's just that I'm so surprised that I ..."

"Well then, make sure you get over the surprise, because the condition is that you have to pass all five exams. And you've only got—*we've* only got—nine days left."

He looked at me, smiling radiantly and gritting his teeth: "I'll show you!"

"Well, let's get down to work!"

He laughed again, moving his arms away. "Fine, but you have to let go of me first, okay?"

I tousled his hair again, shook his head, and once more touched his face with mine so that it tickled. We both almost died laughing as I lifted him into the air and then carried him to the chair. He was next to me, very close to me, as I tidied some papers and lit a couple of cigarettes for us. José began to quickly leaf through the pages of his Latin Grammar, and I happily let my gaze wander over the walls, the lamp, the old, dark-stained cupboard and out through the window into the late afternoon sun.

It was then that I saw her. She was standing by the windowsill of the dining room, which overlooked the same courtyard. It was Ana, perfectly still, giving me an icy stare. I slowly removed my hand from José's shoulder.

"Where can I find that thing about *cum*?" he asked.

Ana closed the window without averting her gaze, then turned around and disappeared in the direction of the hallway.

"Javier, where can I find that thing about *cum*?"

I heard hurried footsteps in the lobby, then the door to the street slammed noisily shut.

"Look in the chapter about prepositions."

"Oh, of course, that's right."

I lit a cigarette. When I laid it in the ashtray I noticed that the previous one was still smoldering.

"Is this where it is?"

I extinguished the first cigarette, squashing it on the bottom of the glass ashtray.

"No, three pages further on. Prepositions with the subjunctive."

I placed my hand on José's shoulder again.

She was wrapped up in my old jacket, and hardly said a word. I chain-smoked and likewise said nothing. The nights were chilly, but from the park opposite my house you could still smell the stagnant river water and hear the croaking of the frogs. Ana and I liked to walk there after our evening meal; there were couples hiding in the shadow of the trees and people taking their dog for a walk. Before we reached the bridge, Ana sat down on the stone parapet and began to look at the yellow streetlights. After a while she turned her face toward me.

"Why did you want me to get my hair cut like a boy?"

I didn't reply right away. "Because I prefer you like that."

"Do you prefer me like that because I look like a boy?"

"What are you trying to say?"

I could see her bottom lip trembling. That always happened when she was very nervous. "I saw you, Javi. I saw you from the window."

"Yes, I know."

"You were kissing!"

"That's a lie." My voice was as sharp as a knife.

"But I saw you!"

"You can't have seen us kissing for the simple reason that we weren't kissing. So that's that."

"So what were you doing?"

"Crying."

"What?"

"There are only nine days left until the exams, and we were both very tense. I got mad at your brother because he hadn't finished a Latin translation, and I said things I ought not to have said. He was really upset, and he put his arms around me. The two of us

33

ended up bawling our eyes out. That was what you saw. And you couldn't have seen anything else because there wasn't anything else to see."

Ana wiped away a tear with the sleeve of her jacket. "Are you telling me the truth?"

I sat next to her and took her hand. "Do you remember what I told you on my birthday, when we got off the motorbike?"

"Yes. That you'd never lie to me."

"Exactly."

She sighed and began searching for cigarettes in the pockets of the jacket. "Well then, just tell me one thing: do you like boys?"

I've just told you I don't lie and I'm not going to lie, I thought. *So if you love me you'll have to take me as I am.* My hands were sweating.

"I like some boys, but not all of them. Just as I like some girls, but not all of them."

"Aha. I understand."

She didn't cry, she didn't scream, she didn't even look at me. She sat quietly next to me with an expressionless face, her gaze drifting off somewhere into the distance.

"Have you ever slept with a boy?"

"Yes, I have."

"With José?"

"No. Not with José."

"Okay." She took a deep breath. "The truth is that I've slept with a girl too."

She said that in a totally calm voice. It took my breath away.

"Does that surprise you?" she asked, smiling.

"Well, yes. I mean … to be perfectly honest the thought would never have crossed my mind."

"And it would never have crossed my mind that you might fall in love with my idiot brother, Javi."

34

"Your brother isn't an idiot. Your brother feels that everyone despises him, especially you, and that makes him suffer dreadfully because he's got such a big heart."

"And that's why you've fallen in love with him?"

"What gives you that idea?"

Ana turned toward me, took both my hands in hers, and looked at me. I could see in her eyes that she was trying her utmost to conceal her increasing anxiety.

"Javi, do you love me?"

"Of course I love you. I love you very much. How can you ask me something like that?"

"And … do you feel comfortable with me? Do you like me?"

I must have put on an evil expression, like some hardened criminal, because Ana recoiled in fright.

"What on earth are you doing? Javi!"

"Come here!"

I pulled her toward me. A few yards away there was a clump of trees where it was almost totally dark. I pushed her onto the thick grass and began to kiss her furiously while I removed her blouse, ripped off her bra, and unbuttoned her jeans and then mine.

"Javi, please, please! You're hurting me! Wait, you idiot! Everyone can see us here."

"Let them!"

"But …"

"Let's see if everyone finally gets the message, starting with you!"

I fell on top of her and penetrated her with one thrust. I heard her scream, but paid no attention. I began to move inside her, consumed by a veritable fury. I held out until I heard her groan; I could feel her arching her back and trembling from head to toe in a long, nervous spasm. Then it was my turn to come. We slumped onto the ground, breathing heavily, while I was still inside her.

"I don't seem to have a hankie with me."

"I have. Wait a moment. It's in my jeans pocket."

Half dressed, we lay in each other's arms on the damp grass, staring silently through the treetops at the starry sky and gradually getting our breath back. Just a few yards away, somebody quickly walked past the stone parapet without seeing us. Ana laid her head on my shoulder and stroked my bare chest.

"Javi …"

"Yes, sweetheart?"

"So you haven't fallen in love with José, is that right?"

The croaking of the frogs became quieter and quieter. In the distance I could hear a siren, dogs barking, and the muffled sound of the river.

"I think I have," I murmured.

"What, Asunción? Salamanca?"

"Of course, with Clara and Pepo, to Clara's parents. But she said she'd told you! My daughter can be such a devil!"

Ana's mother couldn't understand how it was possible for her to have gone without saying goodbye to me.

"It doesn't matter. She'll call me, or I'll call her. Okay, I'll have to be going in a minute, I'm sure José will be waiting for me."

"Yes, he's sitting there studying. Oh Javier, my dear boy, when I think of everything you're doing for him! If it wasn't for you he'd fail again, and I wouldn't know what to do …"

"I'm not doing anything at all. He's the one who's studying, and in any case he has to get through these exams first. We haven't won yet."

"But if he passes it'll all be down to you."

"Nonsense! It'll be down to him! Well, I have to go."

"Of course, Javier, my dear boy. Goodbye!"

Those eight afternoons were almost entirely spent in José's room. On the last night, just hours before his first exam, José was shaking like a sapling in a gale. He had forgotten everything, and was confusing Richelieu with Mazarin, Louis XIV with Louis XVIII, and Austerlitz with Waterloo. The more I questioned him, the more he was gripped by fear and panic.

"Let's start again, Javier. I can't remember anything. I'm completely useless!"

"You're not useless at all! What you need is sleep."

"No, what I need is to go over it all again. I haven't got the faintest idea about the campaign in Russia."

"You know almost as much about the Russian campaign as Napoleon!"

"No, I swear I don't."

"And almost as much as me, because after this summer I think I actually know quite a bit more than Napoleon himself."

He laughed. Seeing him smile, a brilliant idea came to me like a flash. Why did I always think of things when he smiled? "Your exam is at four o'clock tomorrow, isn't it?"

"Yes."

"Have you got your sports bag here?"

"Of course."

"Well then, get it packed and let's go."

"At this time of day? Where to?"

"To cross the Beresina. Without the Russians noticing anything."

José didn't understand. "Where?"

"To the pool. Don't you fancy a dip?"

"But it's half past two in the morning!"

"Well, so much the better," I replied. "The Russians are all asleep at this hour."

He looked at me wide-eyed, shaking his head and smiling open-mouthed. I tousled his hair. Half an hour later we were both in our swim briefs, sitting on the far end of the diving board and smoking a cigarette. Our feet were swinging six feet above the dark mass of water, and there wasn't a soul in sight. We had climbed over the wrought-iron gate and changed into our briefs on the grass. The lamps on the terrace were left burning all night, and cast a feeble light on the distant lawns and the fence. Up here we were surrounded by semi-darkness in which one could only see the glow of our cigarettes. The sky was overcast. José was inhaling the smoke and taking it deep into his lungs.

"Are you okay?" I enquired.

"Sure, I'm absolutely fine."

"Aren't you cold?"

"Cold? Don't be silly. It's not cold at all."

"Good. Then let's begin."

"Begin what?"

"Weren't you wanting to go over everything again?"

"Here? Have you gone soft in the head?"

"You ask me and I ask you. The first person to make a mistake goes for a swim."

José laughed out loud, threw his cigarette into the void and immediately lit a new one.

"Congress of Vienna."

"Good Lord, you ask me that every day," he laughed. "1814."

"The month, José, the month!"

"Oh right. September."

"Good. The man who was behind the Unification of Italy?"

"Hey! It's my turn now!"

"Oh yes, true. Go on, ask me!"

"Hmm … no idea. You usually ask me. Let's see. Lafayette."

I sighed. "Lafayette was a French general who fought for the Americans in the War of Independence. They were really boring people back then who spent all their time praying." I took a deep draw on the cigarette. "A romantic in an era when there weren't yet any romantics, José. An idealist. Imagine Che Guevara in a red tunic with gold buttons. Someone who loved freedom above all else, someone who dreamt about a world where people were— above everything else—happy. Free and happy, José. Someone who would have turned up at the pool at three in the morning to sit with you and me on the diving board."

I drew in my legs and crossed them on the rough fabric that enveloped the thick diving board. I leant my back against his naked back and slowly let my head fall until my neck was resting on his.

"Is that all right?"

José didn't reply.

"Okay, I'll take that as a 'yes'. Let's see … the Treaty of Utrecht."

I felt José put his cigarette to his lips, slowly exhale the smoke, and cough slightly without moving his head away from mine.

"José, don't tell me you can't remember the Treaty of Utrecht."

"You're the best friend I've got," he whispered.

The lights of the city cast their yellow glow on the bottom of the clouds. Far above our heads the wind was rustling the leaves of the poplars. I closed my eyes.

"Wrong answer," I said, and gave José a slight shove in the back.

The splash as he hit the water sounded like a cannon shot in the midst of this nocturnal silence. It took a moment for his head to reappear; he was below my dangling feet, treading water and making circular movements with his arms.

"So what's the Beresina like?"

"You'll find out soon enough!" he snorted. "1713!"

"What are you on about?"

"1713! The Treaty of Utrecht! And we lost Menorca and Gibraltar." He splashed water at me with his hand. "Wait until I'm up there, then I'll show you!"

"You want a fight, eh? Well, get ready Bonaparte, because here come the Russians."

I dived in head-first. The water was surprisingly warm. I was right next to him, and swam underwater in the blue darkness until I finally found his feet. I pulled them down, and he spun around and got hold of my waist. We wrestled for a few seconds. His skin felt like soap under the water. We returned to the surface, laughing and gasping for air.

"And which king was on the throne?" I shouted, maneuvering so that I was right in front of him.

"Where?"

"Where do you think? Here!"

"Um …." He sniffed and shook his head, trying to get his breath back.

"Philip V."

"Shit," I snorted, "you do know everything after all, you jerk!"

I pushed him down by pressing forcefully on his shoulders, and immediately swam very quickly to the other end of the pool. But José could swim like an otter. It wasn't long before he was catching me up, holding my feet, pulling me under the water and winning the race. When I reached the edge of the pool he was waiting for me as cool as a cucumber, his arms resting on the flagstones. We could both stand up, and I placed myself next to him, breathing heavily.

"You may know a lot about history, but I'm better at swimming, eh?"

"That's only because I smoke."

He said nothing. Shortly afterwards he turned to face me. The lights of the terrace were closer now, illuminating half his face, his wet hair, the droplets that ran down his cheeks, and his smile.

"And the answer was correct," he said.

"Which one?"

"The one I gave you," he murmured. "The fact you're the best friend I have."

I smiled. "No, José." My voice sounded calm. "If anything, maybe the second best. Because the best friend you have is yourself."

I saw—guessed—knew—that his eyes were shining. He removed his arms from the edge of the pool, stood in front of me and slowly began to embrace me with one arm around my waist and the other around my neck, gently pressing me against him. I refused to resist any longer. I too began to embrace him tenderly, caressing the skin on his back, which was so soft and slippery under the water. I let my hand roam slowly between his shoulders and his waist without daring to go any further. Suddenly, as I altered my position in order to shift the weight of my body to the other foot, I could feel something pressing against my stomach. José had an erection in his blue Speedos. He noticed my erection too, and stayed completely still. I carried on stroking his back, but getting slower all the time.

"Javier."

"Yes."

"You're trembling."

"I know. So are you."

"Shall we get out?"

I gave a deep sigh, closed my eyes and leant my forehead on his shoulder.

"No."

"It must be around four. What on earth shall I tell my mother?"

Tell her you spent tonight with your arms around me in the water, I thought. *Tell her how you desired me and I desired you, although you didn't dare admit it to me, let alone yourself. Tell her you kissed*

41

me, almost suffocated me with kisses, bit into my throat until I cried out; that you caressed me, that the two of us rolled naked over the grass. Tell your mother we made love underneath one of those bright lights, tell her you love me, that you suffer every second you can't be with me, that you'd die for me. Tell your mother ...

"You're right," I whispered into his ear, "we ought to go and dry off. You've got your exam tomorrow and you need to sleep."

"Listen, we could stay a little while longer if you like."

"No, José." I removed his hand from my neck, tenderly moved him away from me, combed his soaking hair with my fingers, caressed his cheek, and smiled at him: "There's a lot at stake tomorrow. Come on, let's go home. We'll have plenty of time to be together."

We got out of the water and headed for the place where we'd left our bags and towels.

"And I hope you can walk as well as you can swim," I smiled, "because you won't be able to push me under the water in the Picos de Europa."

"Oh well, I have to pass first."

I grabbed his arm and stopped him dead in his tracks.

"You'll pass," I said, holding back my anger, "you'll pass all five exams or I might do something I regret."

"Okay, okay," he laughed, "if you say so."

"I do say so." My tone of voice almost resembled a snarl. "And I mean it too."

We got dressed. On the way to his house we had to cross the park next to the river, and I could see shadows scurrying in the darkness. José didn't seem to notice this. It was ten to five when we arrived at his front door.

"Well, the big day has arrived," I smiled.

"Yes."

"Are you okay?"

"Sure," he smiled, looking into my eyes.

"Better than when we left here?"

"I reckon so." He was silent for a moment, and gave me a gentle tap on the shoulder. "Ana is so lucky to have someone like you."

He was still looking at me; I didn't know what to reply. I took his hand and squeezed it.

"Off you go, Bonaparte," I tried to smile. "You need to rest. The Russians will be up soon and they don't take any prisoners. Quick march, it's time for bed!"

He nodded in agreement. "Until tomorrow, Javier."

"Until tomorrow, my boy."

He stood still as if he was waiting for something. "Aren't you going to wish me luck?"

"No, you don't need it. Go on, get yourself upstairs."

He smiled, waved goodbye in his familiar way, and closed the glass door in front of me. The staircase was illuminated by a weak light bulb, and I calculated how long it would take him to reach his apartment, imagining him climbing two steps at a time as he always did. I walked to the other side of the street, leant against the wall and lit a cigarette. There was a light from his window: one, two minutes, then darkness and silence. I was overcome by an unbearable sense of loneliness, shame, disappointment and longing. *Shit*. I threw the cigarette away. *It's all shit, and I'm a piece of shit too.*

I quickly ran home, opened the front door, hid my bag behind the grille of the elevator, tidied my hair a bit in the mirror that hung in the lobby, and went out again into the fresh night air. I resolutely crossed the street, walked a few yards along the brightly lit avenue, and plunged into the obscurity of the park. Without a moment's hesitation I walked through the dark clump of trees and finally leant against the stone parapet with my back to the river. The lights on the other bank were shining, but they were a long way off. I waited until my eyes had become accustomed to the darkness, then crossed my legs and lit a cigarette.

Here and there, protected by the silence and the darkness afforded by the clump of trees, I began to make out black silhouettes slowly wandering around, occasionally passing one another and sometimes disappearing. One of these shadows seemed to appear from the nearby fence. I watched him move slowly in my direction. As he came past me, just a couple of yards away, I could see him. It was a man of about fifty or sixty, stout and wearing glasses. He smiled at me. I abruptly averted my gaze and looked to my right: there's nothing sadder than a pathetic old man in a leather jacket and tight pants. He stopped a little further to my left, close to the bridge, and leant against the parapet without taking his eyes off me. I carried on smoking.

Another shadow appeared a few minutes later. He passed in front of us, looked at me out of the corner of his eye and likewise made himself comfortable on the parapet, just a couple of yards to my right. He was around twenty, blond, with a long strand of hair that covered his forehead and almost his left eye too. He was wearing jeans that had evidently been ripped on purpose, and you could see his bare chest underneath his denim jacket. He fixed his gaze on the lights of the avenue and didn't even look at me once.

A few seconds passed. I heard the steps of the old man approaching me, and decided to slowly walk over to the younger man. I stood right in front of him.

"Have you got a light?"

"Yes, but you're already smoking, dude."

"I know."

He laughed. I guessed, rather than saw, that he had a handsome face. I had a fleeting impression that I'd seen this face before.

"Okay, okay. But you need to do me a favor, all right? You get the idea. A bit of support, kinda two or three thousand pesetas would do."

His tone was rough, professional and rather offensive. I took a long draw on my cigarette and then threw it away.

"I'm sure you realize that no-one has any money whatsoever on them at this time of night …"

"That guy there is bound to have some cash on him!"

"Who?"

"Him, the one who's after you."

"Okay. In that case you should go and ask him. So long." I turned around and headed for the clump of trees.

"Hey, wait a minute! Don't get sore with me!"

He jumped off the stone parapet and came after me.

"Are you sure you haven't got any dough on you? Nothing? It's just that I'm having a real hard time, dude."

"And I'm having an even harder time. If only you knew!"

He looked me up and down, then turned his face to the left and to the right.

"I'm not into guys, you know."

"Yes, I've already realized that."

"I've got a girlfriend, dude, my chick. But I need some dough."

"Well sorry, buddy. There are plenty more people here, so I'm sure you won't be going home empty-handed."

He stood still, his thumbs hooked into his jeans pockets. "Have you got a cigarette for me?"

I gave him one. When I lit his face with my lighter I could see he was looking at me and smiling. He drew on the cigarette with the intensity of someone who hadn't smoked for hours.

"Have you got somewhere we could go?" he asked.

"No. Have you?"

He was silent for a moment, looking over at the clump of trees.

"Come with me," he said, "there's a place back there."

He set off. I followed him, but made sure I always lagged a little way behind. The place he had in mind was a dark, foul-smelling spot behind a little concrete building that was painted yellow. In front of this building and stretching to the illuminated sidewalk of the avenue just a little further away was a fenced enclosure with a miniature asphalted circuit on which schoolchildren learnt how to handle a go-kart or ride a bicycle during the summer months.

"We'll be fine here, dude." He leant against the wall. It smelt of urine. I stood next to him without looking at him.

"What's wrong? Don't you like me?"

"Sure I like you."

"So? Are you still sore with me because of the money?"

I took a deep breath, turned around and embraced him. I kissed his throat.

"Well! You are the romantic type, aren't you?"

I eagerly stroked his back, his smooth chest, his waist and his shoulders, still kissing him all the time. His denim jacket fell to the ground. I pressed my hips against his and immediately felt his stiff cock. I put my hands in his pants, and his little buttocks suddenly hardened. Then he moved his head abruptly and kissed me on the mouth; I felt his tongue almost pushing into my throat. I forcefully returned the kiss, biting his lips and rubbing them against mine. I rolled my tongue around his, drooled over his chin, sucked on it, then once again pushed my tongue as far as it would go while his nervous fingers undid my shirt and I in turn unbuttoned his pants.

"Fucking hell, dude, you're a real horny kisser. Keep going, you're making me really hot …"

I felt his hand pressing against my crotch, but then he suddenly stopped in surprise.

"What's wrong?"

"I don't know."

The lights on the far bank of the river revealed the look on his face. He gave me a sad smile and then a little kiss on the lips.

"You're thinking about someone else, aren't you?"

I nodded. He hesitated for a moment and then began to stroke my bare chest with the back of his hand, very slowly.

"Shall we just leave it?"

"No."

I felt his knuckles moving over my chest hair, then his hand, and finally his forearm, which instead of caressing me seemed to be amusing itself by roaming all over my upper body.

"As you wish."

I slowly unbuttoned my jeans and let them fall to my ankles, all the time looking into his eyes. I placed my hands on his shoulders.

"Just get this into shape," I whispered, "I'm sure you know how."

He gave me a wicked grin and knelt down. I closed my eyes and immediately imagined José's wet face looking at me in the pool as it had done only a little while ago. The boy carefully took my cock in his mouth, and it was soon obvious that he knew very well what he had to do. His tongue slid very lightly over the tip of my cock and circled my glans. His mouth opened and completely enveloped my penis, sucking on it with a maddening slowness. His nose, forehead and strand of blond hair rubbed gently against my stomach, then moved away again only to return before barely a moment had passed. I could feel the increasing heat and moisture within my body; his hands caressed my ass, which was now as hard as a rock. His lips and tongue occasionally played with my balls and pubic hair, kissing and licking, then immediately returned to engulf my cock. *José embracing me in the water, his stiff penis under his blue Speedos suddenly touching mine, my hands wandering from his neck to the base of his spine: José looking at me, José hugging me tight.*

The boy suddenly coughed and suppressed the urge to gag. "Hey, how much deeper are you planning to go with that?"

"Please don't stop!" My cock, wet with spit, was pointing up at the starry sky.

"But don't come yet, okay?"

"Don't worry. Carry on."

"Goddam, you have no idea how big your cock is. Even though it was a little reluctant at first ..."

He carried on giving me a blowjob, faster now, more rhythmical, all the time fondling my balls. *We could stay a little while longer if you like*, José had said. Why hadn't I dared to? Why did I have to notice his fear, his trembling? Why hadn't I made the move that he had perhaps (perhaps?) been expecting from me? I could see his face. I could see every little bit of his face just a few inches away from mine. How was I to know if he was expecting a kiss while my hand, under the water, was almost imperceptibly stroking his back? I felt my knees giving way, and I started to feel dizzy.

"Stop." I held the boy's head firmly in both hands. "Wait. It's still too early to go home."

The boy giggled and stood up. I grabbed him by the armpits, leant him against the wall, and squatted in front of him. His cock was straight but neither too long nor very thick; it looked like it was about to explode. I began by lubricating his balls with spit, slowly enveloping them, sometimes touching them with just the tip of my tongue and sometimes licking them with its entire length. Then I sank his cock into my mouth. It tasted salty. I gradually began to move my head: my lips enclosed the tip of his cock and then advanced further, pressing like a ring on each tiny bit of skin until my throat sensed something pushing into it and obediently opened wide. Then my mouth slid back and forth, getting slightly faster all the time. I began to stroke his stomach, his chest, his stiff nipples, and his waist; while still moving my mouth, I let my fingers wander over his thighs, his hard little balls, and the narrow space between them and his asshole. I felt his entire body tremble and his hands bury themselves in my hair.

"Holy shit," he gasped, "holy shit."

I wiped away the spit with the back of my hand. "Are you going to come already?" I asked.

"I don't think it would take much."

"And is there anything else you'd like to do?"

We looked each other up and down. "That depends what you have in mind, doesn't it?"

I suddenly grabbed his hips, turned him around, and forced him to spread his legs. I opened up his ass with both hands and plunged in my tongue as far as it would go. He groaned and panted for breath, his cheek and arms pressed against the filthy concrete wall. I furiously slammed my face against the hard, warm flesh and drilled the tip of my tongue into his moist, salty and bitter-tasting hole. Merely dilating at first, it soon became increasingly greedy and elastic. I put my hand around his waist, grabbed his cock and began to masturbate him. I soon noticed his hand holding tightly onto mine, trying to hold me back.

"Take it easy, dude, just take it easy. You don't wanna kill me, do you?"

He turned around, open-mouthed and gasping for breath, and made me stand up. His hair was messed up and he looked much more handsome than before. I shuddered as he stroked my balls; my cock was rock hard. Then, with a rapid movement, he took off his dirty sneakers and his jeans. Now totally naked, he turned his back to me, bent over the parapet with his face toward the river, and spread his legs in front of me.

"Come on, hurry up. But be careful, okay?"

"People can see us from everywhere here."

"I don't give a shit. They can go fuck themselves. The cops aren't around at this time anyway. Go on, but be gentle, and spread some spit on your dick, okay?"

I spat into my hand and once again moistened the tip of my cock as well as his warm and dilated hole. The boy tensed up when I pressed for the first time.

"Careful, dude, careful!"

"I'm being careful. Relax."

Half an inch to begin, then one inch—I moved as gently as I could, but the boy was still very tense. A bit deeper, and deeper still. Once my entire glans was inside his sphincter I grabbed his cock and began to stroke it.

"Go easy, dude, go real easy."

"Don't worry."

I soon noticed him arching his back and gradually beginning to press against me. Quite obviously this wasn't the first time he'd done something like this. He didn't like guys, he'd said. What a whore!

"Go on, a bit deeper. Like that, yes. Not so fast. Holy shit, why haven't you brought any lube?"

"What?"

"Nothing. Carry on. Wait, let me put it in. Just keep still, okay?"

I gradually felt the warmth of his ass enclose my cock, slowly absorbing it, squeezing it, relaxing, and then squeezing it again. My legs were tense and my knees were shuddering violently.

"It's all in now, isn't it?"

"Half."

"Half? Hell, dude, you'll tear my ass open."

I felt my cock beginning to catch fire inside him, and decided to dispense with the niceties. "Does it hurt?"

"Only a little bit."

"Okay. You asked for it!"

"Hey, wait, wait. Wait!"

I took no notice. I grabbed him by the shoulders and thrust my cock further in. His ass opened up like an orange. It wasn't a violent thrust, simply deeper and more insistent, until I felt his ass touching my stomach. He shuddered, and I heard him suppress a scream. I paused for a moment, pushing as far as I could go, motionless; then I pulled it out and penetrated him again, only more vigorously this time.

"Jeez, you're killing me, you're gonna kill me …"

"Would you rather I stopped?"

"Hey, are you crazy? Give it to me!"

I penetrated him deep down with a single powerful thrust, without letting go of his shoulders. I thought I could hear something like a sob. I began to move, to plough through his guts, back and forth, making him feel the full length of my cock, again and again. I was consumed by vengeance and rage: in my mind's eye I could see José watching me emerge naked from the shower, José crying and hugging me in his room, José's erect penis inside his blue Speedos, touching me under the water. *You sonofabitch, what are you so afraid of? Why are you looking at me like that? Why do you have to be so goddam beautiful when you smile? Why haven't you got the courage to love me? Take it, you little shit! Take it! Yes, now! With all the strength I can muster, deep inside your body, until the "I love you" that's sticking in your throat finally comes out of your mouth! Take it, you sonofabitch! Take it, my sweetheart, my love! You can't defend yourself now, there's no escape, not from yourself, not from me …*

"Hey, wait a minute …"

I opened my eyes. The boy straightened up and turned around. He was sweating, and he looked at me wide-eyed and breathless. He took two or three deep gasps, smiled, and with an astonishing agility lay on his back on the stone parapet and wrapped his legs around my neck.

"Grab me by the shoulders, like you did before. But don't push me into the river."

I understood what he was wanting. I reapplied some spit to his asshole, which now opened much wider, and penetrated him without any hesitation. Thrusting energetically, I rammed my cock into him as far as it would go. His hands gripped my shirt, and he looked at me with a tense expression on his face, eyes wide open and with something approaching a smile.

"Jeez, yes, yes, jeez ..."

I plunged into him, again and again. I sensed he was grazing his back on the stone, but I couldn't care less. My mouth still had that taste of salt, blood or fury as I split this small and defenseless ass that was trying its utmost to cling onto me. He let go with one hand and began to jerk off, looking at me all the time. I stared at him as if he were to blame for everything, treating him like a sacrificial lamb, an enemy, a Frenchman on the frozen Beresina who's being run through by the Russian soldiers' bayonets. *José wrestling with me, almost weightless under the dark water, José's slippery skin under my hands, escaping from me, slipping between my fingers like some timid yet smiling fish ...*

"Carry on, don't stop! Go on! Fuck me now!"

The boy trembled, writhed, tautened like a bow, let his head fall back over the black abyss of the river and then pushed himself with a brutal thrust onto my cock. In the half-light I could barely see the fierce stream of semen as it landed on my chest. I paused for a moment. Without leaving me any time to react, he looked into my eyes, grit his teeth, folded his hands behind the back of my neck, lifted himself off the parapet, and clung onto me. My cock embedded itself in his guts as it had never done before; anyone in the park would have heard him scream. Still lifting him off the ground, I turned around, leant against the wall, and made him frantically jerk me with his ass, rising and then falling onto my cock.

"Go on, go on … that's it … kiss me, you sonofabitch!"

I sank my tongue into his mouth. He was naked, clinging to my neck and with his calves resting on the rough stone. He fucked himself with my cock with all the strength he could muster: once, twice, three times, I don't know how often, until I could feel a red flame blazing deep within my eyes and a slow hammer-blow cracking my chest. *You don't know what you mean to me, you don't know what you're doing for me.* A liquid wind scorched my lungs, *my cheek against José's cheek*, a sudden dizziness forced me to open my eyes and my cock plunged itself up to the hilt in this boy's ass, *my cock pressing against José's blue Speedos.* Then I exploded, flooding the boy's abdomen with a wave of anger, revenge, fear and helplessness. His tongue rubbed passionately against mine without realizing it wasn't him I was kissing. The beautiful lock of blond hair covered his face, *José's wet black hair falling onto his forehead*; his fingers were buried in my hair and digging into my neck. He was pressing my mouth against his without realizing that, at this moment at least, his mouth belonged to somebody else. My exhausted hands were stroking this back,,so very similar to that damp skin I had so fleetingly touched, and yet could still feel in my fingertips. His lips detached themselves from mine and began to scatter little kisses all over my face, nose, forehead and eyes.

"You really are amazing, dude!"

My cock was still stiff, and was still inside him. He smiled at me, gasping. "How you doin'?"

"Great. Awesome. And you?"

"Holy shit! You really split me open, but you gave me a damn good fucking. Wait a moment, I'll pull it out now, okay?"

He rested the soles of his feet on the parapet, disentangled himself from me, and was suddenly back on the ground again. He tidied his hair a little, still staring at me all the time.

"Wait, I'll find you a hankie. Your chest is in a real mess."

"Yes, thanks."

I buttoned up my shirt and pants. He gathered his clothes, which were scattered all over the dusty ground, and began to get dressed. I lit a cigarette.

"Aren't you going to give me one?"

"Yes, sure. Sorry."

We both rested our elbows on the parapet and stared at the river. To our right, a tentative blue light was beginning to emerge in the far distance beyond the as yet invisible mountains. I drew deeply on my cigarette. The glow briefly illuminated the boy's face, and I could see his serious expression.

"You really have a crush on José, don't you?"

"Who?"

He drew on his cigarette and looked at me again. "Don't know. You were fucking me, but all you could say was 'José, José."

"Me? I didn't say anything!"

He stared at the river in silence. A woman on the other bank was hurrying up the steps to the bridge.

"It's not very nice being fucked if the guy's thinking about someone else as he does it."

"I'm sorry. Forgive me."

"No, I already knew. It's completely obvious that you're in love. I really don't care, honestly."

The woman had reached the footbridge and was heading for our side of the river. I had the impression she was observing us. I looked at my watch.

"It'll soon be daylight. We should go, shouldn't we?"

"Ah, yes, okay." I detected a sudden roughness in his voice. "So you're satisfied, are you?"

"Yes, totally satisfied, sure."

"Awesome. Can I ask you a favor?"

I smiled at him. I could see he was still serious. A sudden gust of wind made me shiver.

"Okay," I said, "to be honest I do have some money on me. Three thousand pesetas. Is that enough?"

He held out his hand without taking his eyes off me. It was a look that was full of contempt, although I couldn't understand why.

"That's enough." He took the money without looking at it, folded it, and without any further ado put it in the pocket of his denim jacket. "But that wasn't what I wanted to ask you for, dude."

I started to feel uneasy. The woman from the bridge had already vanished. We were alone.

"Nothing. Just leave it."

"No, tell me."

"Doesn't matter, dude," he murmured, ignoring my worried expression. "You got what you wanted, and so did I. We'll be seeing each other again."

He turned around. I immediately grabbed him by the arm. "What do you mean by that?"

"Nothing."

"What do you mean, nothing?"

"Nothing," he said softly, full of hatred. "Let go of my arm, okay?"

I let my hand fall by my side. We exchanged glances that could have cut through steel.

"I just wanted you to kiss me like you did before, dude. You're such a damn good kisser. But I can see you're a sonofabitch like everyone else. I'll make myself scarce. Bye."

He turned around and headed for the bridge. It took me a while to react.

"Hey! Listen!"

He stopped, turned around and gave me an indifferent stare.

I went up to him. He wanted to move away, but before he could do so I took his face in my hands. His slim, agile body, his messed-up hair, his embittered face and tired eyes suddenly seemed very beautiful in the morning light. I smiled at him.

"But that's not the way to do it, sonny."

"What?"

"You kiss as if you were unblocking a sink. Just look …"

Without letting go of his face, I brushed my lips over his: a light, dry touch, hesitant, uncertain, almost undetectable, on his surprised lips, like a butterfly alighting on a leaf. He wanted to open his mouth but I didn't let him. My tongue roamed over his skin, paving the way, playing with his teeth for a split second and then slowly, very slowly setting off for the inside of his mouth and that already familiar taste, the place which had previously been invaded but was now being visited with utter tenderness. His tongue met mine, as if by chance, and the two of them touched each other, recognized each other, exchanged secrets, caresses and gentle touches, playing innocent children's games, all of it so sweet and natural. I suddenly noticed I was stroking his face, which was now his face and not that of another. My fingers hardly touched his trembling ear, the hair falling onto his forehead, his smooth back covered with goosebumps. I kissed his cheek.

"That's better, isn't it?"

He carried on looking at me and smiled again.

"Yes. I think so too. Goddam, you sure know how to kiss, Javi."

The two of us remained motionless, locked in an embrace in the middle of the park as dawn began to break.

"How do you know my name?"

"Hell, because you told me, dude."

"I didn't tell you."

He laughed. "Well, I couldn't have made it up."

We parted. He winked at me and headed for the bridge, still

doing up his jacket. I walked toward the avenue; the yellow glow of the streetlamps looked out of place in the clear light of day. Suddenly I heard his voice.

"Javi!"

I turned around.

"You forgot your smokes!"

He threw the pack through the air. It landed a few yards away from me in the shadow. I bent down, and when I straightened up again the boy had already disappeared.

He didn't even tell me his name, I smiled, *or he told me and I can't remember it*. I crossed the avenue, walked up the grass in front of my house, and arrived at my front door. When I opened it I bumped into the janitor, who was mopping the marble steps. I said hello, removed my bag from its hiding place, and yawned as I entered the elevator. I very carefully opened the door to the apartment because my parents were still asleep. I tiptoed to the bathroom and took a quick shower. A moment later I was already in my room, looking for the last cigarette before going to bed. I suddenly stood still, amazed to find a pack of cigarettes in each of my two pants pockets.

I waited for more than an hour on the sidewalk opposite the school, smoking one cigarette after another, sitting on the steps, standing up, sitting down again, and looking at my watch every thirty seconds. I counted the cars, the streetlamps, and the girls walking past, calculating how long each phase of the traffic lights would last and then smoking again. It was the morning of his last exam. When I recognized him in the midst of the group that was walking along the path in the middle of the courtyard I was on the verge of bursting with suspense. José saw me from a distance and waved at me as he always did without breaking off his conversation with his friends. He was carrying his black briefcase and his dictionary under his arm. I could see he was smiling. *Good omen*, I thought, *although you never know with him*. My heart was in my throat, but I made a poker face and calmly sat down on the little wall next to the steps. He said goodbye to the others when he reached the gate, looked right and left, and ran straight across the street toward me. He greeted me with a light slap on the shoulder.

"Have you been waiting long?"

"No, I've just arrived."

"Yeah, yeah. Liar!"

"What makes you say that?"

The ground was littered with cigarette butts. "Because I'm sure it was you who smoked all of them."

"Oh well, maybe I've been sitting here for a while."

José sat down next to me and took the lit cigarette I held out to him. The little devil was also making a big effort to keep a straight face.

"Right. Are you going to tell me or not?"

"What?"

I took a very deep breath. "José, I'm going to push you to the ground in a second, and the sidewalk here is really hard."

He laughed gleefully. "Okay, okay! Would you like to start with the bad news or the really bad news?"

My heart skipped a beat. "The bad news first. I'd prefer to have a good motive if I have to kill you."

"Fine, so the bad news first. They've just announced two more sets of grades. Would you like to see them?"

"No, you can tell me."

"Wait a second, I can't remember …"

I considered for a moment whether it would be better to throttle him or simply smash his skull against the sidewalk.

"Physics: passed."

"Good." I suppressed a cry, but was unable to conceal the fact that the hand holding my cigarette was shaking. "So that's three out of five."

"But in literature …"

"José, stop fooling around." I leapt up. "They can't have failed you in literature; after all, you knew more about Calderón than the playwright himself."

"Just wait a moment, you're getting ahead of yourself! 'Excellent' in literature. That already means four out of four."

"'Excellent'?"

"Yes."

"Are you sure?"

"Of course, take a look for yourself."

"That's not much, considering what you know," I grumbled without looking at him. José roared with laughter.

"Gimme a break!"

I looked at him. He was radiant. I swallowed and pleaded with the heavens that the world might stop forever at this very moment, with José looking at me with the most dazzling smile I'd ever seen on his face. I recalled his surly, insecure expression, his sour face from the early days of our acquaintance. How he had changed! How was it possible for belief in oneself to alter a person in such a way that it was reflected in their appearance, their face and their eyes, so that day by day, week by week they became lovelier and lovelier? José's beauty was resplendent, timeless, almost angelic, the kind of beauty that can only come from happiness. At that precise moment José was the most beautiful human being who had ever existed.

"And—? Haven't you got anything to say about that?"

I took a deep draw on my cigarette and looked across at the schoolyard with a false air of serenity.

"And today?"

"You might at least congratulate me, hug me or something like that, don't you think?"

I was sorely tempted to deny myself that pleasure. I remained motionless and didn't look at him either

"So how did it go today, José?"

"Oh well, so-so." He leant back, lit another cigarette, and crossed his legs with a look of indifference. "The teacher arrived almost ten minutes late."

"And—? Go on."

"Well, that's ten minutes less for the exam, isn't it, because she said she wasn't going to give us any extra time. Do you think that's—"

"Yes, yes, yes. Go on!"

"Okay. So she came in with her pile of papers and then suddenly had the idea of changing the seating arrangements so we couldn't copy off other people. Another five minutes. Just imagine that, because—"

"José!" I shouted.

"What?"

"So what the hell did they test you on? You'll be giving me a heart attack! Get to the point!"

He was grinning like a Cheshire cat. He threw his arm around my neck and put his mouth very close to my ear.

"Non es eques," he whispered portentously. *"Quare ..."*

"... non sunt tibi millia centum," I continued without a second thought, unable to believe what I was hearing.

"There you are, teacher. You guessed it!"

I stared at him incredulously.

"Omnia si quaeras, et Rhodos exsilium est!" I exclaimed.

"Precisely!"

"Suetonius!"

"The very man!"

"Tiberius Nero! *The Twelve Caesars* of Suetonius!"

"Gaius Suetonius Tranquillus," he expounded, comically raising an index finger and trying not to laugh.

"But José, you lucky sonofabitch, you knew the text by heart!"

"Well, almost by heart."

I seized his hand, which was lying casually on my shoulder. "And what did you do?" I enquired.

"Well, just the translation, the analysis, which was very easy, the historical commentary, signed it, handed it in, and then off I went."

"How long did it take you?"

"Not long. Twenty minutes. I was the first to finish."

I squeezed his hand with all my might, twisted it around, and bent his arm behind his back. He laughed uproariously as he tried to free himself from my grip.

"You sonofabitch!" I shouted, hugging him. "You're a complete sonofabitch! And I'm sitting here all morning, counting fucking cars!"

"I saw you from the window." He looked at me with a happy expression.

"But—then that means—," I buried my fingers in his hair and squeezed his neck. "You've passed all five exams! You've passed everything! You've done it!"

"*You've* done it," he said, suddenly serious. "You helped me."

"No," I said, "I helped you to help yourself. It was you who won the war, Bonaparte!"

"You know very well it wasn't like that, Javier," he said softly, giving me a piercing look with his black eyes. He was smiling. My God, how he was smiling. "Okay. So do I get a hug now or do we have to wait until the grades are announced?"

I stood up. "Come here, you little darling."

He slowly got to his feet without taking his eyes off me and stood in front of me, smiling his brilliant smile and looking as serene as a young god. I threw myself against him, pressing him to me with all my might until the pressure of his chest against mine began to hurt, until there was no longer any room for anything or anybody to come between us. He was there for me, everything was for me and no one else in this radiant moment in which he and I were so alone, just the two of us, the sole inhabitants of the universe. His slender hips pressed against mine, against my boundless joy, my innermost soul, until his smell mingled with mine, until the tears of happiness that streamed from his eyes became my tears, our tears; the two of us alone in the middle of the street, hugging under the merciless midday sun as two people had never embraced before, as no one on this earth would ever be able to embrace again.

"You're magnificent, José," I whispered into his ear. "You're totally awesome."

My mouth immersed itself in the dizzying billows of his hair, moistening it with tears of joy, his arms clinging to my neck with the force of a drowning man who is coming back to life.

"You're magnificent, my little prince."

I lifted him into the air and spun round and round like a top: once, twice, five times, many more, I don't know how many, and his arms holding onto my head were like the fulfillment of my wildest dreams as I became completely engulfed by his laughter.

"Let me go, Javier, you fool, we'll fall over!"

His laughter grew within me, from my innermost core, from the very fountain of my emotions, like a child singing, like the sound of crystal goblets, like an immense and audible joy that overwhelmed me, swamped me, inescapably dragging me away into the open whirlpool of his heart. Once his feet had touched the ground again I kissed him without hesitation, I kissed him impetuously on the cheek and then a hundred, a thousand times on his neck, his ear, his hair, his eyes, until I heard him say: "You're so sweet, Javier, so sweet!" Then he plucked up his courage and for the first time I felt that bolt of lightning on my face, his lips next to

62

my ear, his arms clasping my neck, and then his lips pressed onto my face in a brief, intense kiss which swept me off my feet, forcing me to close my eyes so I wouldn't be blinded with happiness, allowing me to breathe again after so many weeks of languishing, agonizing and dying of thirst at his side.

We remained in this embrace for a while, and I would have given my life to make time stand still.

"Congratulations, José," I said softly to him, my mouth close to his ear. He tenderly stroked my neck and moved his head away from mine.

"Thanks," he answered with a smile, looking deep into my eyes. "Maybe we should go and eat something?"

"Yes, let's go eat. Or rather let's go and celebrate. I'll invite you to a place that—"

"No, Javier," he interrupted, "I'd like you to come and eat at my house today. I want to tell my parents, and I want you to be there, okay?"

I smiled. I could picture Asunción's face, the tears she'd be certain to shed, this proud little woman embracing me, embracing him, constantly taking her glasses off and putting them on again to hide her emotion. She'd scurry through the dining room like a shy but happy squirrel, calling everyone on the phone: *our José has passed all his exams! Did you know that, Carmen? Did you know that, Ángel? José has passed all five exams, yes all five, you heard right! Is Mama with you, or has she gone to bed? Oh what a shame, you can give her the news and tell her to call me when she gets up, okay?*

"Agreed. We'll eat at your house today."

We set off along the upper section of the avenue. He had put his arm around my shoulder and I'd placed my arm around his waist. To our left, the park was shining in the sun. Out of the corner of my eye I could see old people sitting on benches in the shade, people listlessly crossing the park in the direction of the bridge, and a mother holding her children by the hand. I saw the little yellow building beside the children's practice circuit, the metal fence, the little trees wilting next to the totally deserted miniature roadway. The park was a friendly place during the day. For a brief moment I could clearly see the blond boy's face.

"Well, José, a promise is a promise."

"What promise?"

"Shall we drop by at my place and fetch the rucksack now, or should I bring it to you this afternoon?"

He trembled. "But … do you really mean we're going away? To the Picos, you and me? Seriously?"

"With five out of five, eh? That was the deal. And you won!"

"I thought you wouldn't remember."

I could have killed him. "We'll fetch the rucksack after we've eaten. You can pack your things and we'll get the bus at half past nine tomorrow morning. Don't forget to pack an anorak, because you never know up there. And don't weigh yourself down with tins of food; we can buy all that in the villages, in Posada or Cordiñanes."

"Javier—"

"Your sleeping bag is okay, even though it can get pretty cold up there at night. But I'll take the down sleeping bag with me, so there won't be any problem."

"Listen, Javier—"

"What?"

"Well, I don't know. I'm so lucky."

"What do you mean?"

"To have gotten to know you. To have you as my friend, the fact you took so much trouble with me. You're just an awesome guy, really. If it hadn't been for you, then—"

I interrupted him. "What will your mother think?"

"My mother? What about her?"

I tousled his hair. "Well, if you carry on saying things like that I'll arrive at your house with my face looking as red as a tomato. Your mother will think I've got some sort of contagious fever and she won't let you go away with me tomorrow."

He laughed and squeezed my shoulder. "Don't be silly, she'll see you for what you are, won't she?"

"Me? But of course, I'm a saint."

We turned the corner of the square, chatting and laughing. Suddenly José let go of me. "Wait a moment, Javier, I'll be right back."

"What's wrong?"

"Nothing, I'll be back in a second, okay?"

He ran off and crossed the street. A girl with long black hair was standing in the sun on the other sidewalk, waving her arms and smiling at him. I recognized her from the pool. My stomach tightened until it hurt. I saw José talking to her, smiling, raising a hand in front of her face and showing her all five fingers extended. She gave a shout that even I could hear, jumped up two or three times, then flung her arms around his neck and kissed him on the lips. I turned away, shaking. I was standing by the window of a surgical supplies store. Behind the glass stood a plastic head with a bandage on its forehead, a couple of metal appliances, and various boxes of sticking plasters. *Plasters*, I thought. *We must take plasters with us. José is sure to get blisters on his feet.* I looked for a cigarette. I had none left.

Part Two

*D*ozens, hundreds of people; countless bundles, packages, cardboard boxes tied up with string, suitcases full to the brim, plastic bags: early. on a summer Saturday the bus station was something approaching a human anthill. José and I both wore checkered shirts, heavy boots and thick woolen socks. He had chosen jeans, but I had opted for my Bavarian-style shorts which were made of dark blue corduroy. We were laden down with our rucksacks, making our way through this noisy tumult. The line at the ticket office for the bus to the Picos was one of the shortest. We put our bags down.

"Have you got a cigarette, Javier?"

"Sure. Wait—shit, I left the pack at home. I always have to forget something."

"Doesn't matter, I can go and buy some. Do you know where?"

"There's a machine in the cafeteria, on the other side; the tobacconist's here is still closed at this time of day. But hurry up!"

I crossed my arms and studied the wall of dirty green tiles covered with the remains of posters announcing events that had happened many years ago. The big clock was showing twenty past nine, and an illegible metal board displayed the buses' departure and arrival times. In front of me stood an old married couple waiting their turn. She had linked arms with him. He was sporting a faded beret on his gray head and was anxiously gripping a worn-out brown leather suitcase.

"Hi."

I turned around and felt a shiver run down my spine. It was Ana.

"Hi, babe." I didn't know what to say. "What are you doing here?"

"I was going to ask you the same. What are *you* doing here?"

I tried not to look nervous, but fear made my throat tighten. "Have you got a cigarette?" I asked.

She passed me the one she was smoking.

"I'm going to the River Cares for a few days."

"With José perhaps?"

"Yes, with José."

"Okay. And why?"

"I promised him. I told him if he passed all five exams we'd go to the Picos together. And he managed it."

"Wow. That's awesome."

I thought it would be better to ignore her ironic tone. I just nodded. She carried on looking at me, her arms crossed and not even batting an eyelid.

"When did you get back?"

"Two hours ago," she said. "By train. Then I came here for a walk."

"Haven't you been home yet?"

"No."

"The day before yesterday you told me on the phone you wouldn't be coming back for a week."

"Yes, but I spoke to my mother last night and she gave me the news. It seems I have a very smart brother, don't I? And I never even noticed."

The old woman in front of me was looking at us out of the corner of her eye.

"Please, there's no need to raise your voice."

"I'm not raising my voice."

"Okay, you're not raising your voice. Tell me, what do you want?"

"I want you to stay here. I don't want you to go."

"Sorry, Ana, but I'm going. Or rather: I'm not sorry, and I'm going," I said slowly.

At that moment I saw José; his face was pale. He was looking at us from the other end of the hall, clutching two packs of cigarettes in his hand.

"Fine. In that case I'll go with you."

The line advanced by a couple of yards; I dragged the two rucksacks behind me. "You can't go to the Picos wearing moccasins."

"So don't buy any tickets yet. Wait until the three o'clock bus and we'll all go together."

I could see she was on the verge of bursting into tears. I felt terribly sad. "Ana, no. We're going now. I'm sorry."

"Oh, so you're sorry now? But you just told me …"

"I'm sorry that I'm hurting you. But that's all."

"Okay. But what you're—"

"Hi Ani, how you doing?"

José appeared, as white as a sheet and smiling with all his might. He passed me a pack of cigarettes and kissed his sister. She looked at him without saying a word. The old couple in moved away from the counter. It was my turn. Ana grabbed my arm. I said nothing.

"So, how can I help you?"

The guy at the counter was peering at me through his dirty glasses.

Ana tugged at me sleeve. "Don't go, Javi. Please don't go," she whispered.

"Two to Santa Marina," I said.

"Where? Speak up, I can't hear you."

"Javi, please! Please …"

"Two to Santa Marina." My voice sounded hoarse. I took out my money and paid. While I was waiting for the tickets I noticed someone move abruptly behind me, but I stubbornly carried on looking at the ticket seller, desperately searching for a way out of this idiotic situation. Were my carefully laid plans to be thwarted at the very last moment? And in any case, what right did she have to behave like this? *You just went off to Salamanca without even telling me. You hardly got in touch all that time, you just didn't want to understand, you just couldn't admit* ... But how stupid, how pathetic all this would sound. I noticed I was blushing.

"Javier ..." It was José's voice, but I didn't turn around.

"Wait a moment."

"Javier, wait, don't get the tickets yet, it's better if we go this afternoon."

"What?"

"Here you are. Two to Santa Marina."

I took the change and left the counter. I looked around, searching

"She's gone," said José. He had a serious expression and looked very pale.

"So I see."

"Why don't we stay here?"

I showed him the two pieces of printed paper that were clumsily filled out in blue ballpoint pen with that huge, leaning and illegible handwriting that was typical of ticket clerks.

"I've got the tickets. Would you rather stay here?" I asked him.

"I ... I don't want you to fall out with Ana because of me."

"If I quarrel with your sister it'll be our own fault. You've got nothing whatsoever to do with it. If you want to stay, then stay." Why did my voice have to sound so harsh? "But I'm going anyway."

"On your own?"

"No, I'm not going on my own. I'm going with Gaius Suetonius Tranquillo. The book's in my rucksack. I thought I'd check how much you copied in the exam, you naughty boy."

I smiled, and managed to make him smile too. He looked into my eyes.

"I wouldn't put it past you to have brought the book with you."

"That's right." I lifted the rucksack onto my back. "So what about you? Are you coming with me now or are you going to leave me alone for five days with that crushing bore Tiberius Nero?"

How incredibly beautiful he was when he smiled.

"Okay, okay. I'm sure you know best. But don't blame me later on, okay? Ani's already mad enough at me ..."

The loudspeaker announced the departure of the bus for Santa Marina. I took José's arm and firmly pulled him in the direction of the stand. We arrived just in time to stow our rucksacks in the vast baggage compartment. The bus was half-empty. We slumped down on the back seat as the engine started up with two or three sudden forward movements that made the whole of the old metal structure vibrate. I looked for a cigarette.

"Oh no ..."

"What? What's wrong now?

"Nothing. Look who's there."

I looked out of the window; on the other side stood Ana, smiling at me with tears running down her face. My heart leapt into my throat. The bus began to slowly maneuver backwards. Ana stood there with her boyish haircut and her slender arms, smaller, sadder, more helpless than ever, repeatedly mouthing "I love you, I love you," just so I could read it from her lips. She planted a kiss in the palm of her hand and then blew it toward me, smiling and weeping. I placed a finger on my lips and pressed it against the glass of the window. I saw her make a gesture with her hand, asking me to call her. I saw her wave goodbye. As the bus gathered speed and left the station I just about saw her turn around and set off in the direction of the hall, all alone and wiping away the tears with the sleeve of my old jacket.

I turned away. José was smoking in silence with a bitter expression on his face, leaning against the opposite window and watching the trees, cars and people as the bus pulled away along the avenue.

How could you do that? Someone, or something, murmured from some place that was impossible to find within myself.

An hour later we came to a halt in a large village. The driver announced a fifteen-minute stop. José and I got out to stretch our legs and have breakfast. While he was finishing his coffee I asked for a phonebook and found the number I was looking for. "Yes, that's right," they said. "We can deliver flowers to someone's home. Pardon? Are you sure? One moment, I need your credit card number …"

The girl who was dealing with me must have made a very strange face, but she assured me that for the next five mornings Ana would be sent a bouquet of twelve red roses at nine thirty on the dot. People were already getting back on the bus when I hung up, so I left my coffee. José was looking at me, worried.

"Is she still mad at you?"

"Who?"

"Who do you think? Her."

"I wasn't calling your sister."

"Oh right. I got the impression you …"

We sat down again at the rear of the bus. José remained silent, and it seemed to me that he was avoiding my gaze. I felt more and more wretched.

"Sometimes I feel like a complete idiot, José."

He didn't reply, didn't even look at me. He tried to make himself comfortable in the corner by the window and closed his eyes, but the bus was vibrating so much that it was impossible for him to sleep.

"Come on," I said to him. He stretched out along the back seat, placed his head on my thigh, and lay still with his arms crossed over his chest and his eyes closed. I looked at him without saying anything. The mountains were starting to appear through the windows; the road was winding in hairpin bends, and the increasingly strained and high-pitched noise of the engine showed that we were constantly gaining height. José sighed deeply.

"I don't know what's wrong with the two of you," he said, turning onto his side and now laying his cheek on my thigh. "But I do know you're not an asshole."

I stroked his head; two minutes later he was sleeping like a baby.

The bus stopped, and a moment later the engine juddered to a halt. "Hey, Bonaparte! Don't think I'm going to carry you. Wake up!"

José emerged from his deep slumber with the sweet innocent face of someone who doesn't know who or where they are. He looked around and rubbed his eyes.

"What's happening? What's the time? Where are we?"

"We've arrived."

We were the last to get out. While I busied myself with fetching the rucksacks from the baggage compartment José stood open-mouthed with his hands in his pockets, taking in the view. In front of us stretched the Valdeón valley, sparkling in the bright morning sun like a glittering treasure. To our right loomed the high peaks of the central massif of the Picos de Europa, vast and sublime. The gray rock was tinged with blue as we peered through the mist, and the distant mountaintops were scattered with small, inaccessible patches of snow. To our left, the beechwood that covered the entire hillside all the way to Panderrueda was already reflecting the change of season. The leaves were starting to lose their summery green in order to display the full palette of autumnal colors: red, gold, ochre, mauve and garnet, transforming the mountain into a blaze of impossible colors, a sumptuous extravaganza that shimmered in the sunshine. In the far distance the horizon was clearly delineated by the rocky towers of the western massif at whose feet the valley opened out, green and scintillating, its tiny villages scattered like magic dust.

"Well, we've arrived. What do you think?"

José was still staring in amazement. "It's like a fairy tale."

"But of course," I grinned. "Where do you think they filmed *Bambi*?"

He stared at me wide-eyed. "But *Bambi's* a cartoon?"

I roared with laughter, and he realized I was joking. His face reddened as he too began to laugh.

"You're mean. You're making the most of the fact I'm half asleep."

"You'd better wake up now because we've got a pretty long hike ahead of us."

"But it's downhill, isn't it?"

"Yes, yes. You'll soon see what downhill's like here."

We shouldered our rucksacks and set off. Just a little later we were walking through the village of Santa Marina, surrounded by the typical smell of dung, hay and smoke. From somewhere came the muffled clucking of hens. On a wooden bench in front of a stone house sat an old woman, dressed in black from head to toe. She watched us pass and smiled; we greeted one another.

"Are you heading for the path?"

"Yes, señora."

"That's nice. Youth is such a wonderful thing. But you're traveling very light, aren't you?"

"Light?"

"Yes, hoping for fine weather! Be careful you don't get wet, boys!"

"Get wet? With this sunshine?"

"Goodness, I can see you haven't a clue! Just look down there. There'll be rain, I'm telling you. It'll cloud over in Caín this afternoon, you'll see. You boys shouldn't leave it too late to get a roof over your heads …"

José and I exchanged glances, grinning incredulously: it was slightly hazy down in the valley, but an almost scorching sun was burning overhead. We said goodbye to the old woman and carried on. The path gradually went downhill, always following the stream of the Cares. The two huge rocky masses that formed the valley seemed to be slowly approaching one another. I let José walk a couple of yards in front of me, for the sheer pleasure of watching him from behind: his sleek, slender figure, his black hair tousled by the gentle breeze descending from the high peaks, his hands holding the straps of his heavy rucksack. I occasionally caught up with him and pointed out various features of the landscape.

"That mountain there which looks like a cathedral is the Torre del Friero. The cleft rock over there which is in shadow right now belongs to the Horcados Rojos. Two of my brothers received their first communion in the church there, and I played the organ …"

José looked at me with his little eyes, gave me a sweet smile and asked me questions, pointing in every direction.

"No, Bonaparte, you can't see the Naranjo de Bulnes from here, it's behind those mountain tops. You can see it tomorrow."

He paused on bridges to contemplate with childlike amazement the strength with which the waters of the Cares smashed against the rocks and were reduced to a white foam, roaring all the while like some angry creature hurtling toward an enchanted place that it alone, the river itself, knows how to find. There is nothing lovelier than to see the expression of happiness on the face of someone you love. And José was happy.

We passed through Posada de Valdeón without stopping, and bought a couple of sandwiches in Cordiñanes. We paused a little further down at the Mirador del Tombo, an impressive viewpoint from which one could admire the majestic central massif, and noticed with some dismay that the sky was slowly beginning to cloud over.

"Are you tired?" I enquired.

"What makes you think that? Me tired? You're the one who's always lagging behind."

"That's only so I can catch you if you faint."

We arrived at La Peguera, a delightful meadow where a small, ice-cold stream descends from the everlasting snow to join the Cares, and were already covered by a threatening mass of dark gray clouds. The first drops of rain fell on our faces once we had passed the chapel at Corona. We took out our anoraks and quickened our pace. The afternoon light darkened, and in a few moments a veritable torrent opened up above our heads. By the time we could make out the lights of Caín, the last village in the valley, we were completely soaked. Countless rivulets of rainwater ran over José's face, and I could see him shivering with cold. We reached the bar in the village in a sorry state. The lounge was small and lit by a single fluorescent tube, but it was nice and warm, all the same. Three or four locals were playing cards, eyeing us with a mixture of pity and scorn. We ordered two coffees with brandy. José leant his rucksack against the wall and slumped onto a chair, still shivering all the time.

"Well honestly! We should have listened to that old woman."

"She did try to warn us!"

"Hey! My friend!"

The voice hit me like a bolt from the blue. It belonged to Pedro, the old landlord of the bar. He was small and bony, with white hair, kindly blue eyes, and a fulsome smile that revealed his yellow teeth. His enormous hands were rough and calloused, but his firm handshake made it clear he was glad to see me.

"Why on earth have you come here on a day like this?"

"The sun was shining when we arrived in Santa Marina, don Pedro."

"Yes, my lad, but this isn't the first time you've been here. You should know the weather round here is diabolical. And you weren't exactly dressed for it. And this kid here looks like he's got a fever. Who is he? Your brother?"

José looked up at me with a red face and tried to smile.

"No, this isn't my brother, don Pedro," I said hesitantly. "It's … my friend, I mean, it's my girlfriend's brother."

"Ah, I see. What a handsome young man. But he doesn't look well! Let's see my boy, let me feel."

Pedro placed his huge paw on José's forehead and grimaced.

"The boy has really caught a chill, Casilda!"

The old man walked behind the counter and quickly disappeared into the interior of the building. I moved my chair next to José's.

"Are you okay?" I asked him.

"Yes. Well, I'm a bit chilly."

Without thinking, I kissed him on the forehead. The three or four guys who were playing cards looked over at us with curiosity.

"You've got a slight fever, Bonaparte."

"Yes, I think so too. What about you? How are you?"

"I'm fine if you're fine."

José smiled at me with a tired expression on his face. We could hear footsteps thundering down the stairs. The old man reappeared followed by his wife, an enormous woman in her sixties with a squat nose. She was dressed in black and carried a glass and some white pills.

"Well, let's see boys. This is the best thing for a cold, believe you me. Two aspirins and hot cognac. Come on son, get it down in one and you'll feel as good as new in the morning."

José looked at me in fright, and glanced at the old man. He made a gesture of resignation and put both pills in his mouth.

"Come on boy," the old woman said. "One big swallow and you'll soon feel better, do you hear?"

He took a deep breath and emptied the glass in one go, which brought on a dreadful coughing fit. I stood up. The old man began to slap him on the back.

"Take it easy, it probably went down the wrong way, eh lad? Oh well, he's still a child. Is that better now?"

José nodded in agreement and fell against the back of the chair, leaning his head against the wall behind him and closing his eyes. I sat down again.

"And where are you planning to spend the night?"

"Well, we were thinking of pitching our tent somewhere here, in the meadows at the edge of the village, by the river," I said.

"Are you mad?" snorted the old man. "A tent? Is this the weather for camping? Now listen to me: you know where I've got my new hut?"

"No, don Pedro."

"Down by the entrance to the village, just as you reach the spring. It's only just been finished. It hasn't got a door, but at least you'll be sleeping under a roof and you'll be dry. Do you know where I mean? Come on, I'll go with you. Casilda, bring me the umbrella! Have you got a light?"

"Yes, we have."

The three of us went out into the storm, José sheltering under the old man's huge umbrella while I tried to protect the gas lamp from the wind and rain with my anorak. We descended the street to the entrance to the village. The hut, which was set back in a field by the river, was made of stone like all the buildings in the valley and still smelled of mortar, but at least it didn't leak and there were no draughts.

"Take off your wet clothes. And wrap the lad up well. Have you got any blankets?"

"We have everything we need, don Pedro. Don't worry about us."

"Good, good. It's nice here. You know where to find me if you need anything, eh?"

"Don't worry, don Pedro."

"Well then, I'll wish you good night. And listen, you—,"

"Go on."

"Stop calling me *don* Pedro, for God's sake. You're making me older than I really am."

The old man's laughter disappeared into the darkness. I squatted in front of José, who was breathing fast with his eyes closed. I stroked his face; the fever had roughened the skin on his cheek.

"This is your reward for being so smart, Bonaparte."

José half-opened his eyes and smiled at me.

"If you hadn't passed all your exams you could have been at home now in your own bed, warm and dry."

"If I hadn't passed all my exams," he said with a weak voice, "I wouldn't be here with you now, and that's what I—"

A coughing fit prevented him from finishing his sentence. I swallowed. José was able to pierce my heart with one single sentence, with a couple of unexpected words that were uttered in complete innocence. I tousled his wet hair that was falling over his forehead.

"The first thing is to get these wet clothes off. What have you brought to sleep in?"

"To sleep in?"

"Sure. A tracksuit, anything. No?"

"I thought it was going to be warm."

"Well, you'll see." I couldn't suppress a grin. "You'll see what the Picos are like. But it doesn't matter. You can have mine. Come on, take your boots off."

I got the sleeping bags out of the rucksacks; José's was old and far too thin. He was going to die of cold.

"You know what we'll do?" I said. "We'll spread out your sleeping bag as a base and we'll cover ourselves with mine. It's warm as toast. That way neither of us will be cold. Is that okay for you?"

"Sure. Great!"

José finally managed to take off his boots while I got my gray tracksuit out of my rucksack. He pulled his flannel shirt over his head without unbuttoning it; he had goose bumps. When he pulled down his jeans I felt a shiver run down my spine. There they were: too big for him, as ever, with the white drawstring untied, as ever – his blue Speedos.

"Can you pass me the tracksuit?"

"Oh, sure. Sorry. Come on, get dressed. Put these socks on. They're thick and dry. Jesus, if only you knew what you looked like."

"Me?"

"Well, the tracksuit is far too big for you, José. You look like Pedro with his gigantic umbrella …"

He slipped under my sleeping bag and looked at me with a tired smile. Then he slowly let his head fall back onto the rolled up tent that I had laid out as a pillow. He closed his eyes. I undressed in turn, and spread our wet clothes on our rucksacks to dry.

"Are you going to stay like that, in your briefs?"

"No," I said. I had assumed he was already asleep. "I've got a T-shirt here."

"Aren't you going to be cold?"

"Don't worry. I told you my sleeping bag is warm as toast. It's you who's going to be hot in two hours' time."

I put the T-shirt on and lay down next to him. He was lying on his back with the sleeping bag pulled up to his chin, his eyes closed and now breathing calmly. The gas lamp cast a feeble light over his face, which was the very picture of innocence. *Look at him;*

just enjoy looking at him, I said to myself. *Don't destroy the fragile magic of this moment.* I was suddenly certain that this precise moment, this image of José lying next to me with his eyes closed, this sweet and sleepy face, would be engraved on my soul and stay in my memory forever. Whenever I thought of him many years later, just recalling his name would immediately bring to mind this image of José lying next to me, breathing quietly, feverish and sweating, while all I could hear was the rain beating down on the slate roof above us.

"Aren't you going to turn the light out?" he asked without opening his eyes.

"But I won't be able to see you anymore if I turn the light out."

"And why would you want to look at me?" he smiled. "I must look awful."

"That's true," I joked. "You look really terrible. You make me feel slightly nauseous. You look like they've just dragged you out of the Beresina, soaking wet."

He gave a feeble laugh. He pulled one hand from under the sleeping bag and wiped his fingers over his forehead to get rid of the sweat.

"Do I still have a fever?"

"I suppose so," I said without moving. My heart was beating faster.

"Just feel."

I bent over him, sighing, and kissed his forehead for what seemed like ages: once, twice, three times, very slowly, with all the tenderness I could muster. My lips brushed against the worrying heat of his skin; my hands stroked his damp hair, almost without touching him. My mouth, still hesitant, tried to convey to him all the love that was eating me up inside.

"You've definitely got a bit of a fever," I said. "38 degrees, or something like that."

José opened his eyes and smiled at me.

"You know," he said in a low voice. "That's how my mother always used to kiss me when I was little."

"Really?" I blushed. "And what did she do after that?'"

"She stayed with me until I'd fallen asleep."

Don't force him. I heard the voice of reason echo inside my head. *Let it be him. Let it be him who wants to.* But my heart was straining at the leash.

"And how did you kiss your mother?"

The hand that had previously wiped the sweat from his brow was now placed upon my head, pulling my cheek toward his lips. José raised his neck slightly and gave me a little kiss, fleeting and innocent, full of tiredness. Then he let his head fall back onto the improvised pillow.

"But of course you aren't my mother," he smiled.

"No, I'm not."

He turned around laboriously so that his back was facing me, then snuggled against me underneath the sleeping bag, breathing softly.

"But I'll stay with you until you fall asleep."

There was no reply.

"Good night, little boy."

I heard a sigh of exhaustion in which I imagined an indistinct, "See you tomorrow." I extinguished the light and lay on my back.

"Good night, my love," I whispered, certain that he could no longer hear me. I closed my eyes, concentrating my will on listening to the rain beating down on the roof. I could make out the drops, all the drops, every single one of them as they merged together into the storm and fell upon the slates. I separated them out in my head, forcing myself to listen to them one after the other, deliberately, distinctly, one after the other, so that this annoying sound would drown out the clamor, the wounded and anxious scream that threatened to burst its way out of my chest.

Ana's eyes were white and had no pupils, and they stared at me across the courtyard from the dining room window. I was embracing José, although it wasn't José but a figure made of smoke, an intangible specter in whose writhing body I desperately groped around, searching, trying, flailing hopelessly while those lifeless eyes stared at me, threatened me, slowly came closer, suspended in mid-air. I tried to take a step, a single step in the direction of the door in order to escape, but I couldn't move my feet. The white eyes, hovering in the black nothingness, came closer and closer while José embraced me, pressing against me in the dimly lit swimming pool, but suddenly it wasn't José but a huge lizard with slimy skin that sank its fangs into my throat until it drew blood. I was in the middle of the pool, trying to wriggle free, to escape, to swim away, to flee the claws that were ripping my stomach to shreds and to avoid those dreadful eyes that were coming ever closer, but I was unable to move. The black water ensnared my legs like a tangled mess of seaweed, and I fought with all my strength to make a move, a single step, to liberate myself from this agony. Suddenly there was a scream, a savage cry into the void as my feet struggled, as the blazing eyes caught up with me, as the sharp claws grabbed my neck and pushed my head under water, transforming my scream into an explosion of red bubbles that rose to the unreachable surface while the chill of death flooded into my throat.

"Javier! Javier! What's wrong?"

"What?"

"Are you all right?"

"José?"

"You were screaming."

José's hands shook my arm. I swallowed a couple of times and blinked. It was pitch black. The voice was coming from above, and he was kneeling next to me. My face was covered in cold sweat.

"Wait, I'll get the lamp," said José.

"No, it's fine. Don't move."

"You're trembling. What's wrong with you? Are you getting sick now?"

"No, it's nothing. A nightmare. It was horrible, but it was just a dream. Don't worry."

"Okay, I'll put the light on."

"No, I told you. Leave it. It isn't necessary. Go back to sleep, you poor little invalid. Has it stopped raining?"

José crawled on all fours to the entrance of the hut.

"Yes, it's stopped. You can see the stars."

I let my head fall onto the tent that was serving as a pillow. Every bone in my body was hurting, as were my kidneys and my leg muscles.

"The problem is that this sleeping bag of yours is very hot. I'm not sleeping well either, believe me," whispered José.

My eyes were gradually becoming accustomed to the vague light emanating from the entrance to the hut, and they could make out José taking off his tracksuit bottom, throwing it onto a rucksack and slipping under the sleeping bag again.

"Are you sure you're okay?" he asked.

"Yes. Well, I think so."

"You gave me a really nasty fright."

"I'm sorry. Forgive me."

"Tell me if there's anything I can do to help."

"If I have nightmares," I heard myself say, "I sleep better if someone holds me in their arms. Would you mind?"

"Not at all! Come on, lift your head. You were crying out."

He inserted his arm under my neck and pulled me toward him. I laid my forehead on his shoulder and placed my arm around his hips.

"Are you all right like that?"

"Awesome," I said. "What about you? Are you comfortable?"

"Yes."

In less than a minute José had fallen asleep. I was trembling. His arm was wrapped around me and my naked leg was brushing against his. I could feel a burning sensation in my hand; it was lying motionless on his tracksuit at the level of his navel, immobilized by fright and only six inches away from his blue Speedos. Eventually I knew I couldn't resist any longer, that the torture was simply too unbearable and that I would finally start to caress him. The position in which I found myself meant I couldn't even withdraw my hand and jerk myself off to calm down. And besides, I didn't want to either.

A bird was singing outside. I made an effort not to fall asleep, but couldn't stop imagining my hand slipping under the tracksuit onto José's warm skin, inside his blue Speedos. I dreamt that our lips were finally touching. I longed to have my skin next to his; how I wished to experience the joy of pressing his naked body against mine. I fell into a restless semi-slumber in which I dreamt I was dreaming, and in this dream I was dreaming I was struggling to stay awake so I wouldn't touch him, but then I surfaced into a moment of lucidity in which I abandoned the struggle and caressed him without any inhibitions, dreaming once again that I was falling into a deep and dreamlike state …

The sudden sound of coughing made me open my eyes completely. It was already daylight, so I must have slept after all. When I tried to raise my head to see whether José was still feverish I noticed that my hand was on the skin of his stomach and that it was very gently moving back and forth, almost imperceptibly, without the slightest effort on my part, so that one finger was rubbing against the boundary, the longed-for yet dreaded border, the silken outer edge of his Speedos. I had no idea how long I had been doing this for, and I didn't know whether he could feel it either. I thought my heart would burst out of my chest, but from somewhere inside me I could hear a dark voice saying: *You've already come so far, you won't stop here. All it needs is just one step, a single step. Go on, be brave!* José, motionless, still seemed to be asleep and was breathing lightly and evenly. I plucked up my courage and carried on stroking his stomach with all the gentleness and tenderness I was capable of, at first forbidding my fingers to slip down any further. I wanted, indeed had to believe that if José happened to notice anything he would at worst interpret these caresses as the tender gesture of a friend who was concerned about last night's fever, my terrifying nightmare, or whatever.

My hand nevertheless seemed to have a life of its own, and was unashamedly mocking my stupid cold sweat and my fears of a negative reaction. Barely restrained by my determination to wait for him to seize the initiative, it pressed down more and more, bit by bit, almost imperceptibly onto the smooth edge of his Speedos. Right in the middle of this thin line I could feel the place where the white drawstring—untied as ever—emerged from the briefs. My hand rubbed back and forth, each time lingering a little longer, a little more suggestively. The moment arrived when I could no longer prevent it from stroking the fabric beyond the place where the knot ought to have been so that it discovered, touched, and slowly passed over a smooth but unmistakable bulge. José had an erection that seemed to be getting harder and harder. My hand moved closer and closer, ever more obvious and resolute, over the silky surface of his blue Speedos, playing all the while with the tip of what was rearing up beneath his briefs.

But now this was no longer just my rebellious hand. It was me.

Me yielding to the fact that I had obviously gone too far and there was no going back, that there was no longer any point in suppressing the powerful desire that drew me toward him, and that there was no way these ceaseless caresses could still be interpreted as a gesture of affectionate friendship. When, with anxious tenderness, I touched the hairs that barely peeped out of his briefs above his erect penis, José let out a sigh. He was awake; of course he was awake. He had obviously just been pretending to sleep for quite a while, long before my hand, driven by the dream, had begun to caress him. Now we were lying opposite, but not looking at, each other. I knew he was awake, and he knew that I knew. It was now my move in this grueling chess game of the senses. I had to do something. It seemed too crude to simply launch into action, just like that, without even saying a word. But what could I say? Countless idiotic phrases went through my mind. It was me, Javier, his friend who believed in him most, who had helped him so much, whom he owed so much to. I was the one he trusted, paid attention to, valued and admired, and now I was here lying next to him, embracing him and timidly stroking his Speedos. It had never cost me so much effort to string two words together, to force my voice out of my throat.

"It seems you're slightly aroused, aren't you?" I whispered without lifting my head from his shoulder. José took a long time to reply.

"Aha."

"Why's that?"

"Well, it's been quite a while since … well, since I … I shot my load. And now you've started to fondle me …"

I had to stake everything on one card. All or nothing. I breathed deeply and took the plunge, feeling the sweat running down my cheek.

"Would you like me to help you shoot your load?"

Breathless, I counted the seconds that passed in silence. Five, ten, fifteen …

"Okay. It's up to you."

My hand opened and completely covered the stiff and unstoppable muscle that was pushing up his blue Speedos. I stroked it, gently at first and then with all the subtlety I could muster, letting my fingers wander lightly over his balls, his pubic hair which seemed to be seething beneath the fabric, his hard and urgent shaft, his naked stomach and the top of his thighs. Then, without hesitating, I slid my hand under the fabric and grasped his cock with what I idiotically forced myself to imagine was a simple gesture of affection. His penis was on fire. It wasn't too big, but it was a perfect shape and was throbbing between my fingers. I began to move my hand up and down, very slowly to begin with, again and again, gradually getting faster and faster. José remained silent, but I noticed each time that his climax was getting closer and closer.

"Hey, I'm gonna make a mess everywhere!"

Suddenly he sat up, threw the sleeping bag that was covering us to one side, and pushed his Speedos down to his ankles. Then he lay down again and closed his eyes. For the first time I could see his erect penis in front of me. I tried not to look him in the face, and continued to masturbate him using all the tricks I knew.

"Wait a moment, let's do this properly."

I turned around, and without hesitating for one second I took the entire length of his cock in my mouth. José arched the small of his back like a willow branch. I began to suck this quivering piece of meat, to run my tongue over his glans, over the whole length of his slender penis as it grew even bigger. I fondled his balls, repeatedly thrusting his cock into my throat, squeezing it with my lips until it hurt, until it almost choked me, until I could feel his hands on the back of my head tousling my hair and forcing me to carry on, grabbing me by the scruff of the neck and dictating the rhythm he wanted, thrusting into my throat until I felt he would explode at any moment. From then on I seized control again and took his wet cock out of my mouth, prolonging the sweet agony while at the same time dipping my tongue and fingers into the small, taut area of his balls, just briefly, only to return to the trembling tip of his cock which I thrust deep into my throat in one single movement.

"Wait, Javier—wait! No, not ... stop ..."

The first spurt was brutal and boiling hot; then came another and yet another, an endless salvo which scalded my entire mouth, forcing me to swallow as fast as I could while still sucking up and down. *You won't be able to ignore this*, I thought. *You'll never forget this*. Up and down, until I felt the pressure of his hands on my head subside, his muscles relax, his back slump, his head fall back exhausted onto the tent, leaving him lying there almost unconscious with his eyes closed, breathing restlessly.

I sat up and looked at him. He remained motionless for a moment. I didn't know what to do. "Was that all right?" I whispered, uncertain.

"Oh yes," he replied.

Suddenly, in one swift movement and without our eyes meeting even once, he sat up, pulled on his Speedos and stood up.

"I'm going for a piss," he said, and left the hut without any further ado. It was obvious that—for him at least—it was all over. My cock was like a tree trunk and my aching testicles were demanding to be relieved, but it was certain I couldn't count on José for that. Not at that precise moment anyway. I sat down and lit a cigarette. He returned a few minutes later.

"Well then, what shall we do?"

"Whatever you want," I replied.

"No, whatever *you* want." He forced a smile. "You're the one who knows the area round here, aren't you?"

I looked at him and tried to ensure that my face didn't betray the surge of resentment that suddenly rose from my stomach. There wasn't the slightest doubt that José was unwilling to do what I wanted, but I accepted it in a sportsmanlike fashion.

"Okay," I smiled. "The plan is to climb up to Caín de Arriba and pitch the tent there. Then we follow the trail. How's your fever?"

"Fine, it's gone."

"Let me see."

"Not necessary." I thought I noticed him blush, but he was standing against the light and I couldn't see him that well.

"I don't have a fever anymore, honest."

"All right." I stood up abruptly; he saw my erection and immediately looked away. "So let's start by quickly packing our things together. We have to make the most of the daylight."

Five minutes later we were walking through the village again, laden with our rucksacks. It was ten o'clock, and the sun was shining in the middle of a cloudless sky after the previous night's storm. José's hair was unkempt, and he walked open-mouthed staring at the huge rocks that surrounded the village and threatened at any moment to crash down onto it.

"Come on, it's that way."

"Up there? And where are we supposed to pitch the tent?"

I stretched out my arm. "Look where I'm pointing. Can you see the house that's just about visible up there?"

José looked at me, grinned, and furrowed his brow: "Are you crazy? Have we got to climb up there? But that's—"

"The back of beyond, I know. But that's where we're heading."

I felt the blood rushing back to my heart when I managed to smile at him again. I still had the salty taste of his semen in my mouth and my cheeks were still burning with the memory of the snub I'd received after he'd come, but the worst thing was the certainty that something very important had changed. I had finally

92

touched his body, finally felt his cock in my mouth after longing for this moment for months; I had felt his desire, his immense desire next to me and in me. Now something was warning me from deep inside; I was beginning to be trapped by my own recklessness, by my desire or my love. I had crossed a line and there was no going back now. He was no longer mine in the same way he had been yesterday. What had happened could transform us into two people who were quite unlike what we had previously been. I had the vague sensation that the ground was beginning to shake under my feet, that something was slipping out of my grasp. Until then I had been the older man, the teacher, the comforter, the omniscient sage. I was no longer so sure of that now. Now—and this hadn't been the case before—I had done something that required José's forgiveness.

But José himself was smiling at me with that comical expression which said, *You've gone mad. How are we going to get up there?* He was trying to pretend that nothing had happened, almost seeming to suggest we should forget what had occurred so that we could carry on where we had left off the previous evening, so as to restore his happiness, his trust in me. Even though I didn't yet want to believe it, I knew this was impossible now. As I had told myself only a moment ago, I wouldn't be able to do anything if he wasn't willing. But if I colluded with this pretence, if I joined in with this dangerous game of "nothing happened today" I might be able to regain my own happiness and perhaps prepare myself for the moment I had been dreaming of ever since I met him when, thanks to some miracle I couldn't imagine, the gates to his heart would swing open and lay bare the territory that was of course already familiar to me. After all, he had made himself vulnerable several times before. But I would ruin everything if I deluded myself by believing that the morning's events had breached his defenses and I could now indulge my impetuous desire to kiss him incessantly, so I took the cue he was offering me with his innocent smile.

"What's wrong? Can't you get up there with your rucksack, you weakling?"

He laughed. "I can go anywhere you can."

"That remains to be seen," I muttered, almost biting my tongue. Why did José always say things that could be interpreted in a variety of ways? We set off again. I went in front and quickened the pace. The ascent to Caín de Arriba is a goat track, an improbably narrow path hammered into the living rock, a notorious and slippery slope. To the right is the vertical rock face, while barely a yard away to the left is the increasingly deep abyss that plunges down to the river. The stony path climbs up between them. As I walked I adapted the rhythm of my breathing to that of my footsteps. José stayed behind.

"Are you getting tired?"

"No."

"Let's carry on then."

And fuck you, I thought vindictively. When we arrived up there at the little meadow I knew so well, José was panting like a buffalo, his face bright red and sweat running down his cheeks.

"Are we there yet?" he gasped.

"No, we're only halfway there."

"What … really?"

"No, you moron," I laughed. "We've arrived. Come on, we'll pitch the tent. Look for a stone to bang the pegs in."

In ten minutes we had erected our blue and orange tent. José sat on the grass, still damp from the previous night's rain, and began to look at the surrounding landscape. I remained standing next to him.

"Well, what do you think?" I asked.

"Don't know. It's impressive."

Opposite the rocky walls that surrounded Caín de Arriba one could see Peña Santa de Castilla, magnificent and imposing in the distant blue haze and covered with everlasting snow. Slightly closer was Peña Luenga, a mountain that appeared to have been cut with a knife, vertical and menacing. An impossible path zig-zagged up to the heights, up to the freezing caves where the locals left their cheese to mature. A hundred yards away from the remote meadow in which we found ourselves stood the empty houses of the ancient village which, in spite of being at the mercy of time and oblivion, were refusing to collapse. The grass, tall and beauti-ful, was growing everywhere in such profusion that the beeches, the huge oaks and the bracken seemed to be sailing on a green and perpetually moving ocean.

"Come here, I want to show you something."

José approached the enormous rock that marked the center of the meadow.

"What can you see?" I asked.

"Looks like wax, doesn't it?"

"It is wax. It's left over from my last visit. This is where you light a campfire at night and put candles on the rock. We'll do that this evening too when we come back."

José looked at me, smiling and happy. At least he seemed happy to me. I hurried him up. "We ought to be going."

"Already?"

"Sure. What else did you have in mind?"

"Hmm, don't know. It wouldn't be a bad idea to have a bit of a wash, would it?"

I stared at him. "As you might imagine, there aren't any showers here. But the river's down the path. And don't worry, there's no one up here who might want to gawp. We're completely alone. Did you bring any soap with you?"

"I did."

95

"Then I'll wait for you here and I'll go when you come back," I said. "And watch out for the water."

"Why? Is it deep?"

"No, but it's pure ice. You'll see."

Naturally I followed José without him realizing. He arrived at the place where the stream formed a still pool, looked around in every direction, and began to undress. It was the third time I'd seen him completely naked, but on this occasion he wasn't aware of it. I watched José, slender and beautiful, stumbling clumsily over the rocks in the morning sun. He dipped one foot into the water and immediately took it out again as if he'd been burnt, then put it in again, moved a couple of yards further on and bent low in the middle of the transparent rivulet to lift water up to his face: it was like the reincarnation of some ancient god. I had never seen anything so beautiful, so innocent, so enticing and exciting at the same time. It was too much for me, more than I could bear after the morning's frustration in the hut. I took my cock out of my pants and began to fondle myself, slowly at first and then with more energy. José was performing a balancing act in the water, slowly soaping his arms, chest and furtive penis. I noticed that my teeth were chattering. José's hand moved over his ass and balls with breathtaking slowness, leaving behind a trail of soap suds, and I could no longer contain a furious explosion. I ejaculated violently, wildly, rancorously, and the semen which I had held back for such a long time during so many tantalizing moments spurted into the air like a geyser before splashing down onto the stony track just a few yards away from me. José had meanwhile sat down in the stream, washing the soap from his body and oblivious to everything. *You'll pay for that, my boy,* I thought, panting. *I swear you'll pay for that, and it'll cost you dearly.* I slipped along the path, almost on all fours, until I reached the tent. I stopped for a moment at a place from where I could just about still see the pool in the river. José was on the bank again, hastily drying himself. When I saw him dressing I began to tremble again: he didn't put his Speedos back on, but instead slipped immediately into his jeans. The idea that José would spend the entire day naked underneath his worn jeans made my cock twitch again. When he returned to the tent, smiling and shaking his wet hair in the sun, he found me sitting on the grass smoking.

"What was the water like?"

"Diabolical. You were right. But you get used to it after a couple of minutes."

"Okay, so it's my turn now. I won't be long, okay?"

"Okay."

When I began to undress by the water I was struck by an idea, maybe ridiculous, maybe a premonition, that José might be watching me just as I had watched him. I immediately became aroused. I stole a glance at the hiding place where I had stood. I couldn't see anything and there was no movement, but that didn't mean he wasn't there. I slowly undressed with my back to the path: if he was there it had to be somewhere in that area. I slowly undid my shirt, my boots and my pants, then provocatively pulled down my briefs and, completely naked, walked nonchalantly toward the water. It was ice-cold, but I didn't allow myself a single shudder.

I wet my hands and then my entire body, always with my back to the path. Then I began to soap myself: head, armpits, hairy chest, stomach … when my soapy hands reached my cock I turned around very slowly and presented the trees, the rocks, the path, the majestic mountains and, who knows, maybe José, too, with my magnificent erection. My body was flooded with sunlight. I spread my legs, closed my eyes, and gently, slowly began to masturbate, letting the soap lubricate my cock and mercilessly fondling my balls as I imagined José in my mind's eye, with no underwear beneath his jeans. I began to breathe through my nose. I felt strange, an exhibitionist, one of those porn stars who get more aroused if they know people are watching, one of those boys who work in sex shows and masturbate in front of people who are hidden in cubicles, shielded by the opaque glass and willing to give anything to touch what they can only admire. I stood there with my left hand resting on my hip and thrust my pelvis forward, my right hand moving faster and faster along the length of my smooth, soapy cock. I felt wonderfully sleazy, satisfied, wicked, cruel, magnificent and wretched. Seduced: yes. Trapped: yes. A prisoner of my desire, yes, but a seducer too, vindictive as only someone who loves another more than himself can be. I sensed that I was reaching my climax. I half-opened my eyes: there was no sign of José, but I could imagine with total clarity every single step he would take as he walked in front of me throughout the rest of the day, the rhythm of his perfect ass moving freely for me alone beneath those jeans that were too big for him, his cock revealing itself with every step, each time pushing against a different part of his pants. Excited and enthralled, with a sensation that was akin to being drunk, I made sure I was standing sideways on in case he was observing me. Without hesitating I pushed my left hand between my ass cheeks, rubbed two fingers over my asshole, and gently stroked the place between my balls and my ass, masturbating with increasing speed and vehemence. *José, José*, I heard myself say, heard myself think. I didn't know whether I had spoken out loud or whether it was merely the echo of my thoughts buzzing within my ears, just that word, just the unlikely image of José hiding behind the bushes, watching me, swallowing. *José, José, you'll pay for that* … My semen burst forth once more, this time lit by the sun, like some sparkling insect flying out of my very core. I groaned exaggeratedly, deliberately, so that he could not only see me but hear me too. Then, smiling artfully, I caught the last drops of the thick liquid that dripped from my cock in the palm of my hand

and spread it over my chest and stomach, rubbing myself and mixing it with the dark hair and the soap. Then, just as he had done, I lay down in the stony riverbed and began to play with the water, to relax, to rinse myself.

It only took a moment to dry myself, so I began to get dressed. I put my briefs in the bag of dirty clothes and pulled on my pants so they were right next to my skin. *If we're going to play games, then let's all join in,* I said to myself, smiling rancorously. I arrived back at the tent. José was sitting with his back to me, smoking.

"Was I gone for a long time?"

"No, no, it's fine."

"Are you bored?"

"Why should I be bored?"

I put all the bags in the tent, zipped it up, and locked it with the little padlock. "Well, let's go then. You first, because it's downhill now. Watch out for loose stones, they're very slippery at this time of year."

"Yes, don't worry."

"Hey, what's wrong with you? You're trembling again."

"Me? Nonsense. Why should I be trembling? No, I'm fine. Come on, let's go."

We began to descend. I watched him. He was very red.

He had seen everything. I smiled and grit my teeth. He had seen absolutely everything.

We rapidly passed through the village, and after we'd crossed the bridge we immediately entered the gorge of the river Cares. There's nothing but tunnels and dampness to begin with: José stuck his head out of the openings in the rock, marveling at the two huge vertical walls which had been cleft by the river and which rose up in front of his eyes, only about ten yards apart. Then the path emerged into the light and the landscape became truly awe-inspiring. All we had with us was our anoraks tied around our waists, the water bottle, and the camera that I was in charge of. I took plenty of photos: José smiling and peering out of one of the holes that had been pierced in the tunnels; José in front of an enormous piece of ivy that was hanging down from above; José, nervous and suffering from vertigo, on the narrow concrete surface of the bridge which spans a deep abyss at Puente de los Rebecos; José on the bridge at Puente Bolin, throwing stones into the river far below; José against the light in front of the impressive vertical opening of the gorge. José sitting. José standing. José walking: the photo was taken from behind, and I was the only person to see that it showed his lovely little ass moving beneath the blue denim, his bare skin brushing against the seams of his jeans. José from the front, smiling at me.

"Why do you have to make such a stupid face?" I teased, with the camera right in front of him.

"Me? What kind of face would you prefer?" he blushed, then relaxed and finally smiled the smile I wanted.

The walk was more than twelve miles there and back, and it took all day. To begin with we were walking comfortably, looking at the landscape, taking photos, chatting about this and that. Then, shortly before we reached Poncebos, a fiendishly steep hill transformed the walk into something genuinely sporty. José wasn't as used to this as I was, and he was showing signs of tiring.

We drank a coffee in the village bar, which took barely ten minutes. The sun was already setting as we made our way back, walking quickly in virtual silence. We began to notice the late afternoon dampness that was descending from the rocks. I set a quick pace so that we would reach our tent before it got dark.

"Listen, Javier …"

"Go on."

"Why don't we have a rest?"

"Are you tired?"

"Well yes, a bit, but not that much."

"After the next two bends we'll reach the waterfall, and we can fill our water bottle there. Can you manage it, or shall I carry you?"

"I'll manage it," laughed José.

He looked at me again in a forthright manner. Maybe he had decided to ignore what had happened that morning; if so he was clearly being successful, but I knew just as much as he did that there was something between us, a vacuum we had to fill. I was surprised by the calm with which I told myself this, as if it had been another person's voice. There was a lack of tension, my words springing forth without any trace of the fear that had gripped me while I was caressing him in the hut only a few hours ago. We were sitting next to one another by the waterfall.

"Do you think we should talk?" I asked.

"Sure. What about?"

"Well, something happened between you and me this morning. Something that had never happened before. Have you already forgotten?"

He lit a cigarette. "No, of course not. I haven't forgotten."

"And? What are you thinking?"

José smoked, staring at the rocks. "Nothing. I'm not thinking anything. I mean, of course I'm thinking. I mean, it's not worth discussing, is it? Things like that simply happen between friends, don't they? But that doesn't mean, that doesn't mean that—oh well, you know."

"Yes. Have you ever done anything like that before?"

"No, never."

And then it happened. I realize it was an appalling blunder, but I swear the question came from my lips unbidden, innocent and unpremeditated. It was one of those occasions when the head is thinking one thing and the tongue says something different.

"And would you do it again?"

José looked abruptly into my eyes. His expression was calm, but something stern flared deep within it.

"Sure, why not?"

I swallowed. "No, you've misunderstood. I meant—"

"I do understand. And I've told you I don't have a problem with that, okay?" He took a long draw on his cigarette and threw it away. "But for God's sake, don't pull a face like that." He smiled calmly at me and gave me a light clap on the shoulder. "Come on, otherwise it'll get really dark," he said, and stood up.

We carried on walking. It was as if a change had come over José. He suddenly became strangely talkative, laughing and asking me questions about the rocks that seemed to be watching over us, about how far it was to the river, about 'umbrella Pedro' from Caín, joking with me and forcing me to speak. I felt wretched; he hadn't understood me. All I wanted to know was whether it had ever entered his head that he might make love, have sex, or whatever else he chose to call it with another boy—at any point, or with anyone. But my question had been so clumsily put that he had interpreted it as an immediate proposition for tonight, involving him and me. And he had said yes. My pride was in tatters. I was crazy about him, but I swore to myself a hundred times, gritting my teeth with all the strength I could muster, that nothing on earth would induce me to touch one single fiber of his clothes. That wasn't what I was dreaming about at all. I desperately wanted him to love me, but there was no way I would beg him merely to have sex with me. I wanted love, not charity, and I wouldn't settle for anything less.

"Why are you so quiet now, teacher? My God, and so serious."

"Am I being quiet?"

"Wait, I'll take a photo of you."

"But it's far too dark, José."

"Why? With the flash—tell me, does this toy camera have an autotimer?"

The camera, placed on a rock, captures the image: me with an idiotic forced smile, sitting with my hands linked across my knees; José grinning broadly with his arm around my shoulder, his face so close to mine.

"Have you got any candles?"

"Candles? Of course my boy, here they are. How many would you like?"

"Two of the long ones. Maybe three."

"Very well. Three. Anything else you'd like?"

"A bottle of Ballantine's."

"Of what?"

Señora Casilda, a vast presence behind the counter, was somewhat hard of hearing. I tried to drag José out.

"Nothing. Just ignore him. Come on, let's go."

"No, no." José pointed at the shelf. "A bottle of whiskey please, that one there."

"Are you going to have a party, eh? Well, enjoy yourselves. Dear me, these boys. Well now, let's have a look: two cans of mussels, anchovies, bread, cigarettes, the candles, the bottle. All together that comes to …"

We paid. José didn't even wait until we had left the village before opening the bottle of whiskey and taking a swallow that brought on a coughing fit. I was worried.

"Why are you doing that? What do we need the whiskey for?"

"Well, it's like that woman said: we're going to have a party, aren't we?"

"As you wish But wait until we get up there. If you take another couple of swallows like that you'll fall off the path."

"Yes, okay. Listen, where will we get the firewood?"

"What firewood?"

"You said we'd have a camp fire this evening."

I couldn't stop myself from smiling. God damn him, the wonderful little bastard. I tousled his hair and pulled him in the direction of the path that ascended to Caín de Arriba.

"Don't worry, we'll steal some wood up there from one of the winter refuges. The main thing is to set off now, because in half an hour you won't be able to see your hand in front of your face."

"Come on then, you first, eh?"

"No, you go in front, because if you go behind you'll empty the bottle of whiskey all by yourself, you rogue."

The path to the meadow where our tent was pitched was much easier without the weight of the rucksacks. José began to tidy things away while I set off for the nearest hut. When I returned with a huge pile of dry wood the big rock in the middle of the meadow had been transformed into an altar. José had used the knife to cut the candles into little pieces, and had placed them in gaps in the rock; he was in the process of lighting them. He smiled at me with the lighter still burning in his hand.

"Do you like it?"

"It's delightful," I said, and smiled at him, touched. "You're a genius, Bonaparte!"

"Well, it's your turn now, eh?"

Ten minutes later we were relaxing on the grass, leaning against the big rock and watching the flames crackle skyward in the midst of a whirlwind of sparks. Beyond Peña Santa in the west the sky still preserved a feeble trace of violet light. At the other end of the valley, the two big masses of rock that formed the gorge we had just walked through were submerged in almost total darkness.

"Well, are you going to let me have a drink?"

"Me first. We'll take it in turns, okay?"

We drank. José leant his head so far back that his neck laid on the rough rock. He smiled and stared at the starry firmament.

"It's been awesome today."

"Yes?"

"Of course. The path you showed me was the most beautiful I've ever seen."

"You seemed tired."

"Me? Tired?" He grabbed the neck of the bottle and took an interminable swig. "It's just that you're more used to walking faster, but I wasn't tired."

"So how did you feel?"

"Good." He smiled and looked at me. "I was with you."

"Which means …?" I felt a twinge of pain, but carried on watching the frenetic dancing of the flames with a deliberately distracted air.

"It means I always feel good when I'm with you. Come on, pass the bottle. It's my turn. Listen, aren't you really hot?"

"No."

"I am. The fire is amazing, isn't it?"

He took a generous swallow and unbuttoned his shirt. I didn't move, didn't look at him.

"Aren't you drinking?"

"As my father says," I smiled. "Someone in this family has to stay sober. But all right, pass it over."

He gave me the bottle with an uncertain gesture and leant his neck against the rock again. He closed his eyes.

"What do you think of Beatriz?"

I choked. "Who?"

"Beatriz, the girl at the swimming pool. The one with the long hair. The one we had a row about that day."

"No idea. I don't know her."

"But you don't like her, do you? Isn't that right?" he laughed. He was starting to slur his words. "But she's really cool. She's awesome, don't you think?"

I said nothing.

"Don't you think she's awesome? Eh? Her tits—obviously, since you're with Ani …"

"Shall I tell you a secret?"

"If you want to."

He sat up with difficulty and moved closer to me. Our arms were touching.

"Ana can't stand me. She hates me. But I don't care."

"Ana loves you more than you imagine," I lied. "You just need to talk to one another. And I'm sure you do care."

"I don't, I really don't care. Of course I don't care. Because I've got everything she wants. Where's the bottle?"

He grabbed it out of my hand and drank nervously, wiping his mouth with his shirtsleeve. His face was illuminated by the light of the campfire. I saw a bitter smile on his lips.

"So what have you got that Ana wants?"

"I've got you," he whispered, dragging out the syllables, slurring the words and letting his head fall heavily onto my shoulder. "You're my friend. You're here with me. That really pisses her off, doesn't it? You are my friend, aren't you?"

"Sure I am. Come on, José, stop drinking, otherwise we'll spoil the party."

"I'm fine," he said with difficulty. "Oh well, slightly dizzy!" He giggled. "Listen, the fire here is going out. Shall I go and fetch some more wood? Tell me where and I'll get it, really. No, I'll go, stay where you are."

I put a couple of bits of wood onto the fire, which revived in the middle of a cloud of red and white sparks. I watched José take off his boots, socks, and shirt and stretch out on the grass next to the rock. The candles were going out.

"You'll catch a chill."

"I won't. Come here."

I sat in the same place as before. José was barefoot and dressed only in his jeans. He hugged me, put his arm around my waist and nestled his head on my shoulder.

"What are you doing?"

"I won't get cold like this."

"You've drunk too much."

"So what?"

I lit a cigarette and smoked it in silence, looking into the fire. *No,* I told myself. *You're not going to ruin it all again. Not this time.* I prayed to heaven that José would fall asleep in my arms.

"Shall I tell you another secret?"

"Okay, go ahead," I sighed.

"But it's just between the two of us, okay? You mustn't tell anyone."

"No, José, of course not. Go on, tell me."

"But don't tell anyone, eh? All right?"

"Yes, José, I promise. What's it about?"

"Nothing special. But I know someone who's in love with you."

"Yes, Ana. That's nothing new."

"No," he whispered, and rubbed his head against my shoulder. "Not Ana. A boy."

"What?" I laughed.

"A friend from the pool. He's called Miguel. Don't you know him?"

"No."

"Well, in any case, he's crazy about you. He's told me hundreds of times. But I've already told him you're going out with my sister and there's nothing he can do. You're bound to have seen him already. It's just that you don't realize it."

"I have no idea."

José's unsteady hand searched for mine, which was holding the cigarette, and raised it to his lips. I felt him stroke my fingers. He drew on the cigarette and carried on snuggling against my chest, like a child.

"So you can see it doesn't matter to me if my friends like boys, eh? Can you see that?"

No, I repeated to myself, *Don't do it, you mustn't do it. He's drunk. He's deliberately got drunk to give him Dutch courage, so he can hug you like he is now, because he knows you're longing for that, because you've forced him to believe he'd actually like to do what he's doing now. You know he has faith in you, he trusts you. He depends on you. You're the most stable element in his life at the moment and you've blackmailed him, pressurized him. But you won't touch him. Under no circumstances will you touch him, regardless of whether he wants it or not. Let him fall asleep, then carry him to the tent, put him in the sleeping bag and you'll forget this evening, just like he'll have forgotten it tomorrow morning when he's coping with his hangover. He won't remember anything. You'll have forgotten it all. And then life will simply go on: you'll suffer like a dog and he'll finally be happy. So don't touch him.*

A light, weightless kiss detached itself from my lips and landed gently on his head. *Don't touch him! Leave him alone!* My hand brushed lightly against the side of his body, his shoulders, his arm, his chest, in a reluctant yet innocent caress that was more than friendly and almost maternal, sliding up and down his body. *Don't touch him! Leave him alone!* The pleasant warmth of the fire radiated off his skin, and sweat was breaking out on my forehead. My fingers were unstoppable, flagrantly disobeying my will and wandering inch by inch over his arm and then the naked, silky side of his body, only to return to the pleasing landscape of his chest. *José, my love, my darling boy, forgive me.* My tired, irresolute, hesitant

108

head, my last vestige of self-possession refused to caress him, insisted that I mustn't caress him, entrenching itself and clutching at one final scintilla of lucidity. But my hand deceived me, mocking me just as it had done that morning, approaching his nearby body and remorselessly touching his skin, clinging to the fantasy that this touch was still that of a child, of a lizard, of an unquenchable fire, the last token of resistance against the love that overwhelmed me, drowning me like a wave as it fills a hole in the sand. *Stop it, stop it! Don't touch him anymore.* Another tiny kiss that plunged my nose, mouth and eyes into his black hair. Another kiss, and then another.

"No," I heard him say. "Do it like this morning."

"What did you say?"

"In my pants." His voice was almost inaudible. "Stroke me there. What you did was really horny."

I went very red. *Don't do it, don't do it,* I heard the voice from somewhere inside me, weaker and weaker. *Say no, tell him we ought to go to sleep, that we're both drunk, really tired.* My hand advanced slowly and ineluctably along his arm, his side, his stomach, until my fingers reached his pants and began to move back and forth along the waistband, bittersweet, full of desire yet trembling with guilt. My eyes looked on helplessly as my fingers disobeyed me and slowly roamed over José's quivering stomach. My slow caress brushed against the rough edge of his jeans, and his penis stiffened suddenly and violently as a sigh escaped from his lungs, his eyes still closed.

"I've never kissed a boy," he whispered.

"I know."

"Well, I've never done that with a boy. Only what we did this morning."

"You've already told me that. Come on, go to sleep, you're exhausted. Shall I cover you up?"

He opened his eyes and stared at me intensely. The flickering light of the fire meant I could see how the alcohol was clouding his otherwise so radiant gaze.

"What's wrong?"

"Nothing, José."

"So? Aren't you going to give me a kiss?"

"No, Bonaparte," I sighed, smiling at him with an immense sadness. "I'm not going to kiss you."

"What's wrong? You don't want to now, is that right?"

"That's right. I don't want to."

He moved so fast that I didn't even have time to react. He grabbed my neck from behind and pulled my head toward him.

"You're an idiot," he spat out, smiling, with his tongue flickering and his face almost touching mine. "You're a complete idiot."

He pulled my head lower down, grasped it with both hands and kissed me wildly, almost biting me. Our first kiss, the very first. But not like that, my God; our first kiss ought not to have been like that. I suddenly saw red. I angrily freed myself from his embrace, pushed him away, knelt on the grass and grabbed him under the armpits like a rag doll, then lifted him toward me and grabbed him by the neck. His head was wobbling, and his face, lips and confused eyes were only six inches away from me.

"That's what you were wanting," I roared. "But if you're going to do it, at least do it properly."

"Yes, sorry," I heard him whisper.

I slowly brushed my mouth against his dry and trembling lips, gently moistening them. Then I forced him to open his mouth and very slowly inserted my tongue, searching for his. Without further ado José pressed his mouth against mine and almost stuck his tongue down my throat, sucking violently and filling me with saliva that tasted of alcohol. I pulled away from him.

"Not like that. Be gentle."

"Ah."

"And open your eyes."

"It's just that I feel a bit sick," he smiled.

I had to laugh. I covered his lips with small, childlike kisses, each one in a different place so he couldn't guess where the next kiss would land. Then I slid my lips over his and once more thrust my tongue into the warm sanctuary of his mouth. Our tongues searched for one another, found one another, and danced together for what seemed like an eternity. José's inexperience meant he obediently took his cue from me, tacitly following my movements. He really was learning how to kiss, the touch of his lips innocently brushing against mine, our tongues finally meeting in a moist dialog, holding and welcoming one another. My teeth delicately nibbled José's bottom lip while his fingers gently touched my face, caressing my cheeks and my neck, slowly and hesitantly searching for my shirt buttons and then opening them one after the other. His long, slender fingers found my chest and began to play with it, becoming entangled in my dense black hair and then freeing themselves again. His arms encircled my back beneath my shirt without abandoning the kiss, drinking from me and slaking his thirst, slowly drawing me closer to him. Then he stretched out on the grass and made me lie on top of him, constantly rubbing against me with his narrow, silky, hairless and almost childlike chest. His cock stuck close to my stiff cock, seeking it out, inciting it, challenging it through the jeans. Our hips moved in rhythm, pressing against one another in a mixture of pain and pleasure. His nervous, greedy hands caressed my back, traveling up and down it with increasing speed, then suddenly pushed under my pants. José's hands lingered on my firm ass. He stopped kissing me and smiled without opening his eyes.

"You're not wearing any briefs," he said.

"Nor are you."

"Hey, how do you know that?"

I kissed him on the cheek, very slowly.

"I saw you this morning when you were washing in the river," I admitted.

"Aha, so you were spying on me?"

"Yes."

"All right." He coughed, laughed, and finally opened his eyes. "I saw you too. But only very briefly."

"Only very briefly? And what did you see?"

"Well, you washing yourself, soaping yourself and all that, you know?"

"No, I don't know. Tell me."

"It's slightly embarrassing," he laughed, then looked for the bottle and drank lying down without bothering to sit up. A thin trickle of whiskey ran out of the corner of his mouth and then over his cheek. "You jerked off like those guys in the magazines, didn't you?"

"Which magazines?"

"Ha! Miguel has some like that. The waiter from the pool, the one I told you about, the one who's keen on you."

"Yes."

"There's a guy who looks like you in one of them. Well, that's what Miguel says."

"And do I look like him?"

"Well, ha, a bit. You've got a hairier chest of course. And he, well … he has a—well, he has a bigger—hey, you're squashing me! You're really heavy. Come on, lie down here next to me."

I did as he asked. He was still gasping for breath, lying on his back with one arm around my neck, his bare chest rapidly rising and falling.

"Where have we put the cigarettes?"

"Wait, I've got some here."

I lit two cigarettes and gave him one. José lay still, smoking and staring up at the sky.

"Do you kiss Ani like that too?"

A sudden gust of wind revived the flames in the fire. One of the pieces of wood broke in the middle and fell into the embers with a mournful sound.

"No, I don't think so."

"Why not?"

"No idea. It's different."

José took a final draw from the almost unsmoked cigarette and threw it away. Then he sought the hand with which I was holding my cigarette, took it away from me and cast it into the darkness.

"Well, she doesn't know what she's missing."

His hand made a grab for the back of my neck and his lips pressed against mine. This time I let him kiss me. Slowly, hesitantly and somewhat awkwardly his tongue, lips and teeth tried to imitate what I had just shown him. I enjoyed his kiss in the same way you enjoy a glass of water when you're thirsty: down to the very last drop, the very last sigh, the very last ounce of pleasure. Then I moved my mouth away from his and began to gently nibble his earlobe, his delicate neck and his chin. I heard him groan and could feel his body tensing. He sought my hand and once again led it gently to his stomach, the place where his goose bumps disappeared beneath his jeans.

"Go on, do it to me. Just like this morning."

My tongue set off on its travels at the same time as my fingers began to lightly brush against José's skin, moving very slowly back and forth over his waist at the very edge of his pants. Its voyage began at the bottom of his cheek and then wandered liberally over his throat, leaving behind a trace of my saliva. Then came his chest, his delicate ribcage, his virgin skin. I gently bit his nipples, passing the tip of my tongue over those hard and eager buds. I heard a groan

113

and noticed his stomach contract nervously, then suddenly a space opened up between the smooth skin and the jeans, sending out a warm breeze, an urgent invitation, almost an entreaty.

"Come on, do it."

I took no notice. My tongue continued on its journey: slowly, joyfully yet wickedly it moved over his stomach, his sides, the faint path of black hair that led to the depths of his still concealed genitals. Without meaning to, I stumbled upon the moist and salty tip of his cock. He was really nervous, and wanted to unbutton his pants. I gripped his hand.

"No, let me do it," I whispered.

"But I'll come if you carry on like that."

"No you won't. Relax."

My mouth pressed against his jeans. I gently bit his cock through the fabric, pressing against it with my nose and eyes, my entire face caressing the bulge that was trying to force its way through the denim. His balls twitched every time I felt for them with my tongue; I eventually found them beneath the coarse cloth, moistening and gradually soaking it with saliva until it stuck to the skin that seemed to be crying out beneath it. José turned around and fell onto the grass, awkwardly stroking the small of my back beneath my shirt. One button after another, his penis was emerging between my hands like some feverish, impatient creature. I grasped it firmly and slowly licked it from the very tip right down to the balls. José drove his fingernails into my back.

"Shame you haven't got your Speedos on," I gasped.

"What about my Speedos?"

"They drive me crazy." I pulled his jeans all the way down to his ankles and plunged my tongue underneath his balls, kissing them and then biting his thighs. "You drive me completely crazy with your blue Speedos, you idiot."

It was you, it was you. Don't you dare deny it. You were the one who got drunk so you could pretend later on that the boldness and audacity you demonstrated in that cruel and unforgettable moment was just a sham. It was you who immediately took charge, or at least exploited your advantage, particularly at the outset. It was you who stopped me when you felt my lips envelope your cock: "Wait," you said, and simply changed position on the grass next to me, almost naked already. It was you who insisted on placing your stomach in front of my face and pressing your head against my crotch, against my cock which was almost exploding beneath my pants. Without me saying anything, without me being able to suggest or do anything, it was you who ordered me to carry on sucking your cock while you fiddled nervously with my bootlaces, while you threw my socks somewhere into the darkness, while you desperately tugged at the buttons of my jeans and then pushed them down to my ankles. It was you who grasped my cock without knowing what to do next, with the futile determination of someone who grabs hold of a hammer but hasn't yet decided exactly what to hit.

"Tell me what to do, go on, tell me," you urged, slurring your words because of the alcohol.

"You don't have to do anything, José."

"Don't give me that shit. Go on, tell me what to do."

"Just do the same as me."

I carefully took the full length of your cock in my mouth. At the same time I felt a warm, moist sensation on my penis, advancing hesitantly toward my pubic hair. It was your mouth. A violent gag reflex made you fall back, and you hit your head on the grass.

"I don't know whether I can manage it," you whispered with a groan, and then swallowed. "It's enormous."

"Then leave it. Just lie there quietly."

"No way, you jerk. Will you still enjoy it if I can't get all of it in?"

"Of course I will."

"Go on then. Give it to me."

I slowly licked the underside of your cock with the tip of my tongue, from the end of the glans right down to your scrotum. I trembled when I felt you doing the same, just faster and more nervously. Then I wrapped my mouth around your glans and began to slowly move up and down, each time advancing very carefully by an infinitesimal distance. You copied me. I felt an acute pain.

"José, be careful with your teeth!"

"Oh yes, true. Gee, it's just that I can't get it in."

There's no doubt you were a very quick learner; I already knew that about you. You initially reacted clumsily to the increasing speed of my lips on your penis, but subsequently demonstrated considerable skill. Your thighs tensed and you whined like a frightened child when I ran my tongue over your perineum and then licked your balls and slowly inserted them into my mouth.

"No, not that, not that."

"Why not?"

"Because it feels really weird."

"But you like it, don't you?"

"Don't know. It's a bit like being tickled. I don't know if I like it. Then again, I think it's what I've liked best up until now."

"Good. Me too."

I felt your nose, your hot breath, your little lips and your hesitant tongue bury themselves within the dark mass of curly hair that surrounded my balls, licking them somewhat imprecisely at first as if you weren't sure how to mimic what was being done to you. But it wasn't long before you became fiendishly competent, like a debauched teenager who's gradually discovering the precise places within their own body that give them pleasure so they can subsequently search for them, guess their location and stimulate them within another person's body. A thick, urgent droplet fell from the tip of your cock, and I knew I didn't have much time left either. I tore

116

*your pants off in one go, and you did the same to me. I threw my
flannel shirt into the distance and finally, finally we were both completely naked. In one single movement and without leaving you any
time to resist I turned you around, placed you on all fours and lay
underneath you with my face buried between your nervous, helpless
and longed-for thighs. You couldn't move at all: you were swaying—
remember—because you were drunk, uncertain, and you hadn't the
slightest inkling of what I was planning to do with you. I was crazy,
exhausted and angry. My hands separated your ass cheeks and my
tongue delved with one single thrust into your unsuspecting hole,
into your small, intact, adolescent ass, the hole which I had so often
dreamt of and which had enflamed my thoughts for so many endless nights. You screamed, yelled, tensed like a bow, surprised and
defenseless, and threw your head back. "No, Javier, not that," you
cried, pleaded, but it was already too late. You yourself knew it was
too late, you yourself had unleashed all of this. You at least had
some idea what you were risking. "What's wrong?" I asked as I split
your firmly clenched ass with the full force of my tongue. "What's
wrong?" I repeated, and grabbed the smooth marble of your thighs
and then the greedy muscles of your buttocks, parting them with or
without your consent and vigorously piercing your salty and frightened asshole with my tongue. I felt you tense, try to escape, and
then surrender. At first you were afraid, then unsure, but finally you
eagerly pressed and rubbed your ass against my face in a gesture of
lewd and passionate surrender. Yes, José, you did that, of course you
did that. Your ass sought the onslaught of my tongue, my nose and
my entire mouth, which was now hungrily and uninhibitedly biting
your perineum. My face moistened your delicate and excited ass, the
ass I had dreamt of, the ass I had seen moving in the pool beneath
your Speedos, irresistible under the suggestive contours of the blue
fabric. At that very moment your ass was wetting my face with my
own saliva as the tip of my tongue pushed fearlessly and impulsively,*

117

forcing its way into that place where you felt both fear and pleasure. My hands prevented you from clenching your startled ass cheeks. "I don't want to do that, Javier, it's disgusting!" you cried, and at that precise moment I gave a powerful thrust of my hips, lifted my thighs, and crossed my legs behind your neck, firmly enveloping it and pressing your head, your face, your mouth and your tongue toward my ass. My hand grabbed your hair and forced you to bury yourself in there, but you can't just blame that on my strength, José. It was you, remember—and you can deny it at your peril—it was you who threw yourself against me like a shipwrecked sailor who's dying of thirst, like a crazed madman, it was you who pierced my ass with your tongue like some frightened and desperate wild animal, searching for me while searching for yourself. And how good you were at it, you wretch, embedding your face between my ass cheeks and shoving your tongue deep inside me, as far as you could, as deep as your tongue could reach, yet that was what disgusted you, you sonofabitch, that was what you didn't want to do to me my love, my all-consuming love, my little angel. You were eating my ass out like the sweetest whore in the world, and I was eating your ass out knowing that it was all too late now, that there was no going back, that I would never be able to manage without the gritty taste of your ass again. You were held fast by my arms, obliged yet in no way obliged to insert your tongue, move it around, almost twist it within the very depths of my ass, of my blindness, of my innermost trembling, while my cock throbbed—remember—and pressed against your throat, delighting in this contact with the incredibly delicate skin of your neck. Your cock was meanwhile shuddering on my chest, stabbing, scratching and rubbing the black hair that almost enveloped it until I could hold out no longer, until it was humanly impossible to hold out any longer, to desire you even more avidly, to love you even more, until I pushed you away with utter cruelty, cast you aside, sat up, and hurled you onto the grass so you were lying face down, knowing full well you were drunk, nauseous and unable to defend yourself. I knew you were what I would never have wanted you to be: a naked, helpless boy who didn't even have the strength to complain. It wasn't even you anymore, José, my God, forgive me, it wasn't even you anymore, but instead what your affectionate kindness, the whiskey or your sudden drowsiness had turned you, me, or the two of us into. Still, half asleep or semi-conscious, motionless, you looked so beautiful on the grass, as naked as an angel, sweet and perfect beneath the sweat or saliva that glistened on your back by the light of the dying embers. You didn't even notice when I fetched the cream from the top of the rucksack, you hardly reacted when I quietly and carefully began to rub it into your reddened and eager asshole, two fingers moving mischievously between your thighs, moving tenderly up to the warm and vulnerable entrance that protected your innermost being. Two fingers or maybe just a single one crossed the threshold and carried the cream deep down to where my tongue had never penetrated; you arched your back, trembled for just a brief second and sank down again, exhausted, drunk and befuddled. You couldn't see the cruelty, the tenderness, the fear and the merciless ferocity with which I spread the white cream on my cock, smothering its heat, rubbing up and down the impetuous and insistent shaft. I watched you sleeping there, my hands and my cock burning like a volcano, holding back my breath so I wouldn't wake you up.

I carefully spread your thighs, but you didn't move.

I placed my whole body over you, hovering in mid-air without touching you, just my hands and knees supported on the grass.

I placed the tip of my cock in front of your warm asshole. I pressed slowly, very slowly.

You immediately opened your eyes.

"No," you said, startled.

"Keep calm", I whispered close by your ear. "Relax. It'll only hurt a little bit to begin with, you'll see."

119

"No," you whimpered, fearful and urgent. "Not that. Honestly."

I stopped dead in my tracks. You shook me off and turned over. You lay like that in the grass as I sat on your stomach, looking at me with a sadness you could barely conceal behind your unraveling smile.

"Why not?" I asked, gasping for breath, "are you afraid I'll hurt you?"

"I don't know," you said, and slowly closed your eyelids, "but I don't want to."

"But why not?"

"Just because."

I guessed it. I could see it in his face, read it in his eyes that were avoiding me again, recognize it from his smile which was once more hiding behind the protective veil of alcohol. But he simply couldn't lie to me.

"It's because of Beatriz, am I right?"

He said nothing.

"You've slept with this girl, with Beatriz, am I right?"

I already knew the answer, but I wanted to hear it from him, read it on the lips that had just been kissing me so passionately.

"José, answer me, have you fucked her, have you fucked Be-atr—?"

"Yes."

What a fool you are, Javier. You knew it, but deep inside your soul you were like some stupid little boy who still nurtured the secret, crazy hope that he might say no, that it might not be true, that he would at least have the decency to lie to you so that you could force yourself to believe it too.

I smiled. "And what was it like?"

"Good."

120

I felt the muscles in my face tighten.

"Are you mad at me?" he enquired.

I didn't reply. Sitting on top of him and looking deep into his eyes, I smiled cruelly at him and then put one hand behind my back and grabbed his cock. He almost seemed prepared for what I had in mind. He closed his eyes and sighed.

"So it was good with Beatriz. Awesome. I'm glad. But let's just see how you like this."

I smothered my hand with cream and began to masturbate him, spreading the cream over the entire length of his penis, which immediately became completely hard again. I placed two creamy fingers into my asshole and began to stretch it. It would hurt, and I knew it. I had barely done it two or three times in my entire life, but I hadn't forgotten how. The pain was the least of my worries. This was a contest I had to win.

"Keep still until I tell you."

José didn't move when I placed the tip of his cock in my dilated hole. I took a breath, closed my eyes and very slowly slid down. I paused for a second when I felt José's glans penetrating without difficulty. I pushed the glans into the hole two or three times on its own, then pulled it out again. José was whimpering like a puppy, breathing heavily through his nose and digging his fingernails into the grass. He was enjoying it. It didn't matter who he might be thinking of, he was enjoying it. He suddenly tensed his lower back and pushed up forcefully. It was as if a red-hot poker had been thrust inside me. I bit my bottom lip so hard that I could taste blood; I only just managed to suppress a scream, but the darkness in front of my eyes turned a fiery red.

"Don't move, goddammit. You have to be careful."

"Okay."

The macho little shit. I filled my lungs with air and did a quick mental recap: *Push, push down without relaxing, press with your*

stomach, press with your guts as if you were wanting to empty every-
thing you have inside you onto him. Open up and press!

And that's precisely what I did. I grit my teeth and pushed as slowly as I could, deeper and deeper, gradually going in and out. The pain brought forth tears that burned my cheeks, but I guessed, hoped, knew it would quickly subside. *Go on*, I told myself, *not much further to go, you'll make him die of pleasure and he'll make you die of pleasure. The red-hot poker will soon disappear, carry on, push down onto him.*

"Javier, don't we have to—"

"Be quiet. Are you enjoying it or not?"

"Hell, of course I am. What about you?"

"Not yet. Give me a minute."

Suddenly I felt something within me relax, surrender and cease its resistance. The pain, the cold sweat, all of it was suddenly transformed into a warm wave that rose from my ass to my eyes, lips, and perspiring brow. I had done it. I slowly but surely sat on José's throbbing cock. I felt him rushing into me, easily making his way inside me, plunging right inside me, setting me on fire, making me shudder. The skin on my arms and back became aroused as I noticed the tickling of his pubic hair on my thighs. The full length of José's cock was inside my body. We'd done it, we'd done it, my gauche little boy, my love, my hesitant executioner. I rose and fell, now pressing, squeezing his entire cock with my sphincter, up and down.

"Go on, move."

"Doesn't it hurt?"

"Move! Go on!"

José tensed every muscle in his body and gave me a mighty thrust, and paused again. He looked into my face with a mixture of terror and longing.

"Is that all you can do?" I asked.

122

"I … I don't want you to …"

"Go on, you sonofabitch," I exclaimed. "Get a move on. All that whiskey and so much fuss and now you're as meek as a convent girl. Give it to me!"

He went bright red; I had never seen such anger in his face. His first thrust was fierce, forcing me to raise my face toward the starry sky. I imagined I could almost feel the tip of his cock in my stomach. When I sensed that the next thrust was imminent I pressed down at the same time as he pressed up. I did likewise the next time. José's cock was inside me, going in and out with furious rage, burning my insides, inflaming me with something that wasn't merely pleasure, joy or revenge, and making me go completely crazy. I can't recall what I was thinking about, what kind of cruelty and hatred was going through my mind at that moment. I remember adapting my movements to José's increasingly fierce and uninhibited onslaught. I remember clinging to his shoulders, then leading one of his hands toward my cock and forcing him to grab hold of it. I was about to explode.

"Come on," I said, still moving all the time, still pushing down and squashing him onto the ground. "This time you won't ignore me like you did this morning, you sonofabitch."

José didn't move his hand. Impulsive and uncompromising, he carried on sticking his penis into the very core of my being but wouldn't masturbate me. He merely opened his eyes and looked at me. His flushed face bore an expression of intense pain and bitter indignation, like a child before it starts to cry.

"Don't say that," he gasped.

"What?"

"Don't insult me!" he screamed, his voice faltering, and then he stopped moving. "I love you."

I was stopped dead in my tracks and went as white as a sheet, but I didn't allow his cock to slip out of my ass.

"You … what?"

"You heard."

"But you love Beatriz," I stammered.

"And you, for fuck's sake." He threw his arms around my neck, coughed, and looked at me uncertainly. "And you. Can't you tell? What else do I have to do to make you feel comfortable with me, Javi?"

He gave me a clumsy, slobbery kiss. His mouth smelt terribly of alcohol, and his face was full of tears.

"Come on," I smiled.

I took his cock out and lay on top of him, entwining my arms and legs around him and kissing him all over. He did the same to me. *That ought to have happened sooner, you swine*, I thought. And suddenly there was the old dream of rolling around in the grass with him, hugging him tight, feeling his engorged penis pressing against mine, both of us naked and uninhibited like two willing accomplices; his soft skin against my sweat, longing to have him cling to me, embrace me with much more than his arms alone. I was lying on my back on the grass with José on top of me. We could hardly see each other in the darkness. The big rock upon which all the candles had long since burnt down now lay between us and the campfire.

"Say it again."

"What?"

"That you love me."

"Sure, Javier, of course I love you."

I hugged him and kissed his neck. He was covered in cold sweat.

"Do you really mean it?"

José's head swayed and fell against my shoulder. He couldn't stay upright. "Yes I do. I love you."

He seemed to revive when I lay face down on the grass, spread my legs and forced him to stretch out on top of me. We were once again next to the faint heat of the fire. I didn't have the slightest trouble moving his cock toward my asshole.

"Go on!"

José tentatively led his cock toward the place that eagerly awaited it. It was getting soft again, but a thrust from my gaping ass was enough to put it where I wanted it.

"Let's do it."

José gave two or three feeble thrusts. My ass lifted toward him, pushing itself onto him, urging him on, determined:

"Go on, go on. Fuck me!"

The effect was immediate. José caught fire, and his blazing cock stiffened within my ass. His fierce thrusting was frightening.

"What did you say?"

"Fuck me."

His hands caught hold of my armpits, scratched my shoulders and bit into my arms. José began to move inside me like a suddenly awaking madman.

"You want me to fuck you, eh?"

"Yes, but properly. Fuck me harder. I don't even notice it like that."

"Then tell me, ask me. Ask me to fuck you."

"Fuck me, my love! Go on, harder!"

José thrust furiously into me, then almost completely removed his cock so that just half an inch was left inside me. He then threw himself onto me with all his might, his lance drilling into me with such strength that my chest was rubbing against the grass. Then he pulled out of me completely, his moist cock looming menacingly for a moment in mid-air, but then immediately almost ripping me apart, sinking once more into my very core like a sword, like a vicious fist that made me cry out in anguish.

"What's wrong?" he grunted. "Is it hurting now?" His mouth was close to my ear.

"No, José, it isn't hurting," I sobbed, I laughed. "Stick it in till it hurts." I bit my lips, almost in pain, almost in distress, but definitely with pleasure. "Fuck me properly, my love," I whimpered. "Fuck me! Properly! Yes! Harder, Bonaparte, fuck me, fuck me! My love, my precious little darling!" I begged him, ordered him, and his cock split my insides, his perfect cock cleft my innermost being like some unyielding piece of bone.

"You like it when I ask you, don't you?"

"Yes, it really turns me on when you tell me what to do."

"Well then: fuck me! Rip my ass open, José, Josito! My love, my little darling, finish me off, come on, destroy me."

I could hear José groaning as he tugged at my shoulders, I could hear his wordless commands as his cock plunged into my ass and his arms lifted me off the ground with a hitherto unknown strength, his feet forcing me to kneel down. We both stumbled and I tried to stand up, but a single, simple, powerful thrust of his hips drove his cock into the middle of my soul and made my arms fall flat onto the big rock. My left hand plunged into the burning flame, into the liquid wax of a candle that hadn't yet been completely extinguished. It hurt, yet was almost pleasurable. My right hand scraped against the stone and my body was pinned to the rock. The skin on my chest, stomach and thighs started to tear, and my blood slowly began to drip onto the edges of the powdery limestone while José stood there terrible and merciless, piercing me with all his might, grasping my shoulders and nailing me to the rough stone as he sank his cock into my ass with incredible violence. *"Take it!"* he shouted. *"That's what you were wanting,"* he groaned. *"That's why you dragged me up here."* He crushed me against the uneven rock, thrusting violently with his entire body. *"Now you're getting it, now you're getting it. Isn't that what you wanted?"* His voice was slow, mellifluous, and cruel, and his words were like some strange nightmare. *"Yes,"* I whimpered, *"give it to me!"*

Splinters of rock pressed into my wounds and my blood trickled slowly over my chest, my stomach, my erect penis and my tensed thighs. *"Fuck me! Fuck me now, crush me, tear me apart, my love!"* My hand let go of the rock so that my entire weight and the full force of José's attacks were now born by the sharp-edged stone that was tearing my skin. My hand seized my cock and began to move quickly and frenetically, but José suddenly pushed it away. He grabbed my cock as if he were wringing a bird's neck and moved it brutally back and forth, synchronizing his attacks with the hesitant rhythm of his hand while gasping and snorting through his nose. *"Tell me to fuck you; I love it when you tell me to fuck you. Go on!"* So I asked him, begged him, ordered him, almost screamed at him: *"Fuck me, impale me, go on, harder!"* José was snorting more and more, inhaling deeply and then exhaling again.

"Are you coming?"

"Yes!"

My semen gushed out of me like a torrent, flooding onto the cruel rock, the grass, and his hand.

"Tell me you're coming, go on!"

"I'm coming, José, I'm coming! Fuck me again! Fuck me, goddammit!"

With the first rattle, the first groan, the wounds on my legs, stomach, chest and arms were hammered even harder against the rock. Then came the second, and José plunged his cock into my ass from behind, almost lifting me into the air. A bestial grunt emerged from his throat. I could vaguely feel something warm flooding my insides, searching for a way down, sliding down towards my legs like a balm. There was a third blow that I hardly noticed. José remained standing for a moment, a few seconds, clinging to my shoulders and still inside me. I think he kissed the nape of my neck. Then he withdrew and collapsed.

I took his lifeless body in my arms and carried him to the fire.

I poked the embers and repositioned the half-burnt wood; the rapidly reviving flames revealed that José was as white as a sheet. I sat next to him and took him in my arms, always ensuring that his head stayed upright. He was drenched in sweat.

I looked for my shirt and covered his chest.

"Take it easy, my boy," I whispered into his ear. "Rest, relax."

"No, I'm fine."

"Yes, I can see that. Come on, close your eyes."

I kissed him several times and bathed my lips in the cold sweat that covered his brow. He moved one hand and laid it on my thigh. Almost immediately he lifted it again and studied it.

"What's wrong with you?" he asked.

"Me? Nothing. Why should anything be wrong? It's you who's collapsed."

"But you're bleeding."

"No, it's nothing. Don't worry."

"I've hurt you, haven't I?" he sobbed, trying to look at me even though his eyes were unable to focus on my face.

"You made me see stars," I smiled. "First of all because it hurt like hell, but then later on because of everything else that happened."

José tried to sit up, but when he lifted his head I could see that his stomach was heaving and he was looking distraught.

"I think I need to be sick," he said in a feeble voice.

I lifted him up, put his arm around my shoulder and more or less dragged him to the edge of the meadow. He was trembling like a child. I bent him forward and supported his soaking forehead with my hand. That was all it required. José vomited, retching violently. I covered his back with my shirt. When his knees gave way I lifted him into my arms again and carried him to the tent.

"I've ruined everything, haven't I?"

"Don't talk nonsense," I smiled.

"You won't be able to stand me tomorrow after what I've just done."

"I'll love you hundreds of times more tomorrow than I do today, you moron."

I laid him on his sleeping bag and covered him with mine.

"I'm cold."

"I know. Quiet now. Go to sleep. I'm right by you."

"Wait. Give me a bit of water. My mouth is on fire."

I wanted to hold him upright but he wouldn't let me. He did his best to crawl on all fours to the entrance to the tent, then rinsed his mouth with the water bottle and fell to the ground. I laid him down again and lit the gas lamp so it would burn with a tiny flame. Then I took some alcohol and a clean handkerchief and went back to the fire. It was worse than I had feared. I had torn my skin to shreds and was still bleeding from at least ten or twelve wounds, while the blood had already dried on the others. The alcohol burnt like hell, but it stopped the bleeding.

At least these wounds will heal, I told myself. The others, the ones in my heart, would under no circumstances stop bleeding. That was for sure. I looked for a cigarette. A gust of wind made me shiver with a mixture of cold and fear, happiness and longing, anxiety and joy. It was all over now. I was trapped. Finally trapped. This most beautiful of boys who was sleeping beneath my sleeping bag with the hangover to end all hangovers was not merely my love but my absolute master. There was nothing more I could say, and I no longer had the strength to cope with, control, manipulate, watch out for or indeed want anything else. I was conscious of the appalling madness of love that ruins and destroys life and renders it pointless, painful and agonizing. I was certain that my willpower, however determined it might be, would be utterly routed when faced with the love I had finally obtained only a short while ago. I was left sitting by the fire, naked and smoking a cigarette as I contemplated the flickering of the dying flames. *Well, what are you going to do now?* I asked myself. *You're trapped, lost.* I tried to defend myself: *he told you he loved you.* That was true. But it was also true that he'd lied. I would never be able to forget the image of Beatriz stroking her hair in front of him at the pool, the vision of Beatriz gently and complicitly kissing him on the mouth right in front of me in the middle of the street. I furiously rejected the notion that he and Beatriz had shared the same tenderness that we had just experienced. *He doesn't fancy boys*, I heard myself think. *He did that because* … I forced myself to dispel these clouds of anxiety … *because he loves you. He did that because he loves you. After all, he told you himself.* I was doubtful again: *he was drunk.* But then I was overwhelmed by the stubborn idea that would save me and allow me to sleep that night: *he told you. He told you he loves you.* The doubts were banished, frightened away, fleeing in the face of my terrible determination to cling to his words: he had told me he loved me. What more could I ask for? What more did I need to be happy? I had to be happy. And yet up there in the fantasy world of the starry sky I thought I could make out the constellation of death, dancing before my very eyes.

I don't know how long this agony lasted. I know it was well past midnight when I heard a noise in the tent. I looked around: José, naked and with his hair in a mess, was staggering toward me.

"What are you doing?"

"Nothing. Smoking. Waiting for the fire to go out."

"Come on."

He took my hand and pulled me into the tent. He told me to lie down on the sleeping bag and made me stretch out my arm, then lay on his side with his back to me and snuggled against me, almost pressing his head against my shoulder. My lips, my tiny kisses, the wounded tears that flowed from my eyes took refuge in the tousled black hair on the back of his neck. Then he groped for my other arm in the darkness and wrapped it around him, laying my hand on his cold chest. He pushed his shivering ass against my stomach, and his cold feet sought the warmth of mine.

"How are your wounds?" he asked.

"Everything's fine, my love," I said. "But why are you doing that? Why are you holding onto me like that?"

"Because I also sleep better if someone's hugging me," he said.

Part Three

Are your legs feeling heavy?"

"Yes, a bit," he smiled.

Two days previously we had walked downhill from the viewpoint at el Tombo with our hands in our pockets, kicking away the stones to amuse ourselves; now, in the opposite direction, it had turned into a horrible ordeal. In front of our eyes, legs, and dusty boots the badly asphalted path snaked cruelly upward, yard after yard, with no obvious break or end in sight.

José had woken before me that morning. We were both naked and had become tangled up: his face pressed against my cheek, his hands wrapped around my back, my arms underneath his armpits, and his legs intertwined with mine. I was beginning to wake up myself when he released himself from this embrace and, without saying anything, went to the river to wash. I immediately drifted back to sleep, calm and contented, but José soon returned and shook me awake. I looked at him, still somewhat drowsy. We both had rings around our eyes and were completely exhausted. I took ten minutes to smarten myself up and we went for a coffee at the bar in Caín. Pedro said goodbye, emotional as ever, wanting us to come back as soon as possible, and then we set off. José was in a serious mood. Poor boy, what a hangover! Nevertheless, I was barely able to wipe the smile off my face.

"Tell me, Javier, where are we going today?"

"To eat? We'll get to Cordiñanes, pitch the tent and then devote the afternoon to getting some rest because we're shattered, aren't we?"

"But … if we made an effort we could get to Santa Marina."

"Santa Marina? Our final destination? Are you crazy? Why should we inflict that on ourselves?"

"Don't know. To save time, don't you think?"

"But José, that's one helluva trek, laden down as we are. Moreover, if we already reach Santa Marina today it'll only have been four days instead of five. That wasn't what we—"

"Let's walk to Santa Marina. I think I can manage it. What about you?"

I stood still.

"So you'd like to be home again tomorrow?"

"Don't know. Yes. We've already seen everything, haven't we?"

One day less. One day less with him, *with him*. But ultimately he was right; we had already seen everything. We carried on walking. I had barely had three hours' sleep. You could see José had a hangover simply by looking at his face: he was exhausted. Nevertheless, he climbed. The last mile of the ascent to el Tombo was excruciating, but José grit his teeth and walked as if the ground beneath his boots was on fire. I didn't understand what was happening. It was already past midday when we arrived in Cordiñanes, where we stopped to eat a sandwich. It was the same bar where we'd taken a break when descending the same path. I took my beer onto the terrace outside. Before us lay the impressive panorama of the western massif of the Picos, blue and gray, with its unreachable summits. José joined me and stood next to me, looking at the silent crags.

"What are you thinking?"

"It's beautiful. Really."

The first clouds of the afternoon, sparkling in the sunlight, were beginning to gather around the distant mountaintops. I said nothing for a while. But he was with me.

"Do you know something?" I said.

"What?"

"I'll never forget these days we've spent together. Never in all my life. One day I'll write something about all this. And you'll be there looking over my shoulder and reading it, paying attention to what I'm writing to make sure I tell the truth."

José remained silent, looking at the peaks. "Okay, so you'll let me read it then?"

His casual indifference cut me to the quick. No, it wasn't possible. He was tired, so tired. He had drunk so much last night, the night we'd spent together. I quickly scanned my memory for a common reference point.

"Do you remember what we were studying a few days ago? Literature, sixteenth century? *If I had never seen your face …*"

"Nope. What was it about?"

I turned toward him, smiling:

If I had never seen your face
I would not have suffered so,
yet neither would I have seen your face.
Seeing you has caused such pain,
not seeing you would break my heart.
I would not languish so forlorn,
Yet would have lost much more."

José looked clueless. "No, I don't remember."

"Well, if that had come up in the exam—" I whispered without taking my eyes off his as he stared into the void.

"But it didn't come up," he grinned contentedly. "Listen, have you finished your beer? Why don't we press on?"

We shouldered our rucksacks and set off. He went in front. "Hey, José …"

"What?" Why was he avoiding my gaze? *Why was he avoiding my gaze*? Well, it was obvious: he was shattered. He was so tired. I had to wait until he—

"Nothing. Carry on."

137

"What's wrong with you now? Shall I carry the tent?"

"No, it's fine. Carry on," I murmured. "I'll carry it. The worst is yet to come."

Mussels, tuna, cheese, cockles, some salami, tomatoes we'd bought in Caín, hard-boiled eggs I'd prepared with salt, oil, paprika and oregano: it was a veritable feast—all the food that had been meant for two days in one single meal. We were leaving; we only had a few hours left, barely one more night. We had camped in a hollow a hundred yards from the place where soon, at daybreak, we would catch the bus that would take us home again. Dusk was already falling behind the beech woods of Panderrueda and the countless treetops were shimmering in the last rays of the afternoon sun. José was holding a piece of bread in his hand, staring intently at the light as it slowly faded. *The final light of the final day*, I thought as I watched him.

"Perhaps you should finish your meal," I told him in a low voice.

I loved him so much, so very much at that precise moment as he looked at me for a long time, smiling so sweetly and naturally and finally conceding the little smile I desperately needed to sustain me. His tender face, his beautiful eyes gazed endlessly into mine after an interminable day during which he had barely deigned to look at me. I hadn't been able to see myself in him, know I was part of him, hadn't felt alive in the only way that was possible for me now: in him, through him, and only for him. I had spent a never-ending day during which I had failed to expel from my very core the vile miasma of fear, the ominous murmur which, serpent-like, had been coiling itself around my heart since dawn: *he doesn't love you, it was a lie, he doesn't love you.* But of course he loved me, it went without saying. It was true, wasn't it? Wasn't it? It was written in his eyes, in the light of his eyes which I was finally looking at, which he was letting me look at after a whole day of unbearable torture. I hadn't been able to plunge myself into them, seek refuge, bathe in the gentle warmth of his eyes when he looked at me as I wanted him to, as I needed him to if I was to carry on breathing.

I finally smiled and felt revived. I lit a cigarette and looked across at the distant mountains, seeking his hand with mine.

"Can I have a cigarette?" he asked.

"Sure. Here, take mine."

"It's just that I don't have any left."

"That's fine."

"Why don't we go down to the village and buy some? You've only got two left. Shall we go?"

"It's bound to be shut already. It's best if we just go to bed. Come on."

"But it's only ten o'clock. I'm sure it's open. Come on, I'm not going to leave you here."

He stood up and began to walk. I followed him with a painful sensation of thirst in my throat. The bar in the village was open, full of people, smoke and the smell of firewood. José asked for two packs of cigarettes.

"My goodness, who have we here? It's the boys from the other morning!"

We laughed. It was the same old woman from the day of our arrival, which already seemed so long ago.

"Well? Did you or didn't you get soaked that afternoon?"

"Well, a bit, yes," replied José, laughing.

"You see? I told you, didn't I! Well, well. And what will you be having?"

"Nothing," said José smiling. "Thanks all the same, but we're going now."

"A whiskey," I said. "On the rocks."

"I don't have any ice, young man." The old woman looked at me.

"Then without ice. It doesn't matter."

José made a strange face. "Are you going to have a drink?"

"Sure, aren't you? We're already here, and we're leaving tomorrow."

"I'd like a tonic water please," he said, suddenly serious.

The old woman placed two glasses in front of us. I downed my whiskey in one. The old woman looked at me with an amused and sympathetic expression.

"You're thirsty, eh?"

"You have no idea, señora,"

"Of course I do. It's a very bad path. Would you like another?"

"Why not?"

An hour later I was staggering back to the tent. José went in front, and neither of us said anything. We descended the steep incline into the hollow. José opened the tiny door in the orange fabric and lit the gas lamp, then pulled off his boots and carefully spread the two sleeping bags next to one another. By the time I had just about managed to undo my laces he was already lying in his sleeping bag, the zipper pulled up to his throat and wrapped like a mummy. I put on my gray tracksuit top, which still smelt of him, and lay on top of my own sleeping bag. His back was turned toward me.

"You'll freeze like that," I said. "Why don't I cover the two of us with my sleeping bag?"

"No, I'd rather you didn't. And in any case it isn't that cold; it really isn't necessary."

I touched his shoulder. "José …"

"What's wrong?"

"Come on, look at me."

He turned halfway to face me, and I thrust my lips at his. He abruptly turned away, and his shoulder hit my chin.

"No," he said. "That's enough."

"But what's wrong?"

"That's enough!" he sobbed, almost bellowed, twisting around and turning his back to me again. "I've done it twice. That's enough, isn't it?"

I stayed still for a moment. It couldn't be true. It was impossible. It simply had to be impossible. I threw myself at him without a second thought, fell onto him, hugging him violently through his sleeping bag and kissing him greedily on the neck.

"Let me go. Come on, let me go!" His voice was shaking with fear and anger. "Didn't you hear me? I don't want to do that again."

I let go of him.

"I heard you," I said, shivering. "Yes, I heard you. But why?"

"Because … because I don't like it."

"Why don't you like it?"

"Because I'm fed up with it. I don't like it."

"And what about last night?"

"Last night meant nothing. I already told you that on the way back. It doesn't mean anything at all to me. Above all, it doesn't mean I'm like that. I did it because you wanted it. Just because of that."

"No," I replied. My stomach was tied up in knots, and I was in pain. "You did it because you wanted to. You know that only too well. And yes, it does mean something. You said 'I love you' hundreds of times."

"I said that because you asked me to. That's all. And I was drunk."

"You got drunk on purpose to overcome your fear, José, so you'd have the courage to do what you wanted. It was you who persisted, not me. You're not going to tell me now that you—"

"Hey, you can think what you want."

"What I want to think, what I can't stop thinking is that you told

141

me you loved me. That's what you told me, José. You repeated it so many times, José, you must remember."

"I don't know. I really had drunk too much. I don't remember anything like that anymore. If I said that to you then what I meant was that I love you as a friend."

"That's a lie. That's not true. That's not how you said it."

"Oh well, you can think what you like."

Why was he doing this to me? I briefly wondered whether this might be a sick joke that would suddenly dissolve into a hug or a new flood of kisses. But that didn't happen; the opportunity had passed. I could hardly hold back my tears. That was the moment when, searching frantically inside myself, I came to the terrifying realization that I no longer had any refuge or safe place I could return to. The past had ceased to exist, and there was no going back to the days of the private lessons, the pool and the exams. The Beresina had been a mere figment of my imagination, and we had become different people.

"Hey—" I whispered. "José, at least look at me, come on."

He turned around. There was so much hatred in his stare that I forced myself to lower my eyes.

"Don't look at me like that."

"I'm looking at you like I always do."

My God! When had this "always" been? I felt intimidated by the rancor, the contempt of this stranger who was only waiting impatiently for this conversation to finish so that he could finally get to sleep, but I at least tried to remind him that there had actually been a "last night." I would be satisfied with that.

"José, I don't know whether or not you remember, but last night you were completely happy with me."

"But didn't you notice that every time I touched you I had to think of a girl in order to get excited?"

That was a lie, but it didn't matter now. Everything was lost

142

in any case. Tears began to flow gently and effortlessly from my eyes. Kind-hearted José would have rushed toward me and comforted me; this guy in the tent with me didn't even bat an eyelid.

"A specific girl or just anyone?"

"That's none of your business."

It didn't hurt. If somebody treads on your hand, it only hurts when your first finger breaks; after that it no longer matters whether it's just one or all of them. The old Javier wouldn't have wasted one second in leaving the tent so he could spend the night in the open air, but the little bit that remained of him scarcely knew what to think. All he knew was that the stranger lying next to him in this sleeping bag bore José's beloved face.

"Well, I didn't need to think about anyone apart from you," I said softly. "Because I love you. I believe I love you, José, and I'll never forget last night because there's no one else in the world—"

"And what abou—" he interrupted me, his voice growing louder. "What about Ana?"

Touché. "I don't know. I suppose there are different ways of loving people. But I'm not certain."

"What is certain though is that you must have planned everything, eh?" His tone of voice suggested he'd been waiting for a very long time to spit this out. "The whole pretence of the private lessons—it was very convincing. And all you were wanting was to drag me up here for that."

"For … *what,* José?"

I was accustomed to the radiance of his smile, so this appalling and scornful expression on his face really frightened me.

"You know better than I do, don't you?"

"José," I whispered, giving him a penetrating stare. "José, do you really believe that all I wanted was to sleep with you?"

I think it was only then, in the half-shadow, that he could see the tears dripping off my chin. He said nothing for a while, his head lowered.

"Well, I don't know."

"I'm absolutely certain that you do know. I'm not sure what's wrong with you today, why you're doing this to me, why you're trying not to remember anything of what happened last night—"

"No, it's not that …"

"— but I know you, you're my friend, you're not nasty enough to have forgotten all those things we've experienced together since we met, José. Hate me if you want to, do what you want to me, but don't try to twist what you and I have always felt."

"I was feeling one thing while you were planning something different."

"That's an outrageous lie."

"No, it's the truth."

"That's an outrageous lie!" I screamed. "I was your best friend, you said so; *you* couldn't stand me being angry with you, *you* embraced me that night at the pool like no one had ever embraced me before, *you* were so happy with me the other day when you came out of your Latin exam, *you* loved me yesterday, José, *you* told me that you loved me. You made me teach you how to kiss! What you're saying is a barefaced lie!"

He stayed silent for a long time with his eyes lowered.

"Come on, stop crying."

"I can't."

I thought I detected some indication that he was moved, or at least that he was calming down. I believed I might begin to recognize him again.

"And what's going to happen now?" I asked.

"Now? When?"

"From now on, once we're back."

144

"I have no idea. How should I know?" he lied. "But I believe it won't be that easy for me to forgive you."

"I haven't asked for your forgiveness," I exclaimed. "And I'm not planning to either. There's nothing you have to forgive me for."

"What about my sister, eh? You're deceiving her and yet you have nothing to be sorry about?"

"I've never deceived your sister, nor you. Both of you know that very well. And I'm going to forgive you for what you're doing to me. I have no choice, I love you too much."

"Okay, as you wish." He turned around abruptly and extinguished the light. "And now let me sleep, okay?"

"José, please—" I placed one arm on the part of the sleeping bag that was protecting, indeed shielding his shoulder.

"We have to get up early. Go to sleep now, you idiot."

"José.— José, for God's sake! José, please—"

He turned around like a man possessed. "Don't you realize I can't do otherwise? That I don't want to either? Leave me in peace!"

I don't know how long I stayed sitting on my sleeping bag, disorientated and unable to move, only listening to the death knell of my heart without even having the strength to cry. I tried to see some light in the impenetrable darkness that was spinning slowly in my head and looming all around me. Then I was overcome by a feeling of total exhaustion, so I lay down. He wasn't asleep.

"José," I said very softly.

"What?"

"Till tomorrow."

It took a while for him to respond.

"*Adiós.*"

A little kiss, placed in my hand, flew in the darkness toward the sleeping bag in which he had enveloped himself.

"I love you."

There was no reply. Night finally closed over me.

We sat apart throughout the journey and didn't exchange a single word. There was no one else in the bus. After an hour's rattling along the road José lay down on the back seat just as he had done previously, but a whole century had passed within the space of four days. On the way there he had slept with his head on my thigh. Now I forced myself to look at the countryside through the burning acid of the tears I could no longer hold back. Just the idea of having to move away from where I was made me tremble with fear.

The bus station was practically dead when we arrived. We fetched the rucksacks from the baggage compartment.

"Will you wait for me a minute?" I said. "I'm going to make a phone call."

"Okay, I'll go outside."

He turned around and began to walk in the direction of the exit. That was the last time I saw him for many years.

I walked to the phone booth. Ana answered. She could immediately tell from my voice that something was wrong.

"Hey, what's the matter?"

"Nothing. Are you at home?"

"Yes, sure."

"Good. We'll be right there."

"Listen, what's wrong? Aren't you well?"

"No, I'm not well. Who else is at home with you?"

"No one. My mother is working this morning and everyone else is away. But aren't you going to tell me what's happened?"

"I will soon. We'll come to yours first."

I hung up. When I returned to the hall I couldn't see José anywhere. He'd gone. I grabbed my rucksack and began to walk to Ana's house. I felt absolutely worn out, and the rucksack was almost breaking my back. The four staircases I had to climb at Ana's house seemed like they would never end. It was as if I had aged by thirty years over these four days. She opened the door.

"Javier, what's happened to you?"

"Is he here?"

"He arrived and then locked himself in his room. He didn't even say hello. Wait, I'll go and tell him you're here."

"No!" I held her firmly by the arm. "Leave him. Don't call him."

"But—could you perhaps explain to me now what has happened? Come in first, we'll go to my room. And take that monstrosity off your back."

Ana's room was overflowing with red roses: on the little table, at the head of the bed, on the desk, on the floor. *It looks like someone's died*, I thought.

"The last ones arrived half an hour ago. There are hardly any vases left in the house." She smiled and gave me a kiss on the cheek.

"Some more will be arriving tomorrow. I ordered five days' worth."

I started to feel nauseous.

"Come on, sit down. Wow, you're really pale. Are you all right?"

I didn't move. I stood looking at the flowers, in every corner, one by one, until my gaze settled on Ana's face. I tried to smile.

"Thanks," she said. "They're lovely, Javi, but I think you slightly overdid it. You didn't need to. There are some things I can understand without my bedroom being transformed into a diva's dressing room, okay? Now tell me everything. And since we're on the subject, you know I love you very much, Javi, no matter what's

147

happened. Come on, sit with me, come here. You don't have to—
hey Javier, what's wrong? Are you crying? Are you finally going to
tell me what's—Javi! Javier!"

The first fit of vomiting bent me double as I tried to open the
bedroom door on my way to the bathroom. I don't remember the
second one.

The months dragged by. I was out of hospital within a fortnight,
but the acute hypoglycemia took longer to get better due to the
added complication of the anemia and, above all, because I was
depressed. My parents and brothers didn't leave my bedside. Ana
spent all the time she could with me. Then her classes began and
her visits became increasingly infrequent, but I can hardly remember any of that. The nervous attacks that mainly came over me at
night erupted into fits of screaming during which—as my father
told me much later on—I would endlessly call out for *"a certain
José"* and mercilessly hit out at anyone who tried to approach me.
These attacks were alleviated by way of tranquilizers that for most
of the time kept me in an almost lethargic state. I found it difficult
to clearly distinguish between faces, the different times of day, or
what I was saying and what others were saying to me. Food of any
sort provoked immediate fits of vomiting. All my clothes looked
far too big on me when they finally took me out of this blue and
white room in a wheelchair.

Then I spent weeks at home sitting in an armchair, looking out
of the window, reading or dozing. I saw the poplars in the park
gradually losing their leaves; I saw how people on the street were
wrapping up more warmly; I saw the first desperately sad rains
of the impending fall. Even now it hurts whenever I think how
pale my father was that night when, worried at hearing my steps
in the hallway in the early hours of the morning, he pushed open

the bathroom door and dragged me out of there with the veins on my left wrist bleeding copiously. I had a look of self-absorption on my face which took him months to understand, although he immediately forgave me for everything. Back in hospital I was on medication again, plagued by insomnia as well as the unbearable feeling of loneliness that forced my friends and family to stoically spend almost every hour of the day at my side.

Nevertheless, the nightmares and nocturnal panic attacks became less frequent with every passing week, as did the crippling, intolerable fear of being alone and the vertigo that prevented me from leaning out of even the most innocent of windows. The plethora of drugs began to produce results, although like everything back then it was very slow. The doctor eventually decided that, even if I didn't approve, it was time for me to go out, initially accompanied by my parents or a friend: just short walks, always linking arms with someone, to the cathedral to listen to the organ playing or to the bullring and then back home again. Over time I was able to manage a couple of hours walking and even sporadic trips into the countryside, together with visits to friends, my music teacher, and the faculty. Ana had taken it upon herself to register me while she was in the process of applying for a transfer to Salamanca. I couldn't tell you when we stopped going out together, whether we ever got round to discussing it. I remember that we started to only see one another at weekends, then just occasionally because she didn't come home from Salamanca every weekend. Eventually, when it was already really cold outside, someone told me they'd seen her on another guy's arm. I can't recall what I thought or said, but I don't remember it causing me any pain.

Christmas was just around the corner when they finally let me go out on my own. The truth is that I didn't really know where to go, apart from my psychologist every two days or my music teacher's house in the afternoon. Then my mother surprised me on Twelfth Night with a strange, heavy package.

"Your face is so pale that you look like a writer from the Romantic period," she laughed. "So I've had this made for you."

I was stunned. It was a black cape: not the traditional Spanish cape with a collar and red or green lining, but a genuine priest's cloak that almost came down to my ankles. It was lined with black silk and fastened at the neck with a silver buckle.

"Are you poking fun at me?"

"No, not at all." She was still looking at me, creased up with laughter. "The day you have the courage to go out wearing it I'll know that you're all right again."

She gave me a kiss and tousled my hair as she had always done when I was small. My father was leaning against the wall in a corner of the hallway and observing the scene; he smiled contentedly. I immediately donned the vast weight of this fabric, slung it over my left shoulder and removed my right arm from the ocean of black. There was something comical about the scene.

"See, you almost look handsome like that," she said, curtseying. "Now all you need are some tight pants and some black pointed shoes like your father wore to his wedding."

I went to drink some wine with Paco and Eduardo, the brothers of Ana and José. I was able to smile again, and my face almost hurt; it was the first time for ages that I'd smiled.

It must have been the last week of January, around five in the afternoon. The sky was gray and there was a cold, light wind that promised snow. I was on my way to my grandmother's former house to play the piano that had been my parents' proper gift to me on Twelfth Night; the cape had merely been to make me laugh. This was where they had installed my desk, my bookcase, my computer and everything I needed. As I went out of the front door I could see him on the other side of the street. He was dressed in a denim jacket with a lambswool collar, and I initially had the feeling this was a face I was vaguely familiar with. When he raised his hand and waved at me I took a closer look. Yes, I had definitely seen him before: the hank of blond hair that fell over his left temple, his bright eyes. He was sitting on the stone balustrade. I crossed the street.

"Do we know one another?" I smiled.

"Don't you remember?"

"Well …"

"You gave me this in the park over there last summer. I wanted to give it back to you."

He pressed three thousand peseta notes into my hand. I looked into his eyes. The boy was trying to smile, but he was very nervous. Of course I remembered him: the prostitute from the park that night. I was confused.

"What are you doing here? Why have you come after such a long time?"

"You'll see."

"And how do you know where I live?"

"Well, I followed you when we met," he said without looking at me. "And I've come to see how you are. I heard you were ill."

"A bit. I'm better again now. Thanks very much."

"You've lost a lot of weight."

"Oh well, it's not that bad." I looked at him again. "If I'm perfectly honest, you're the last person I—"

"Yes, I can imagine. Well, if I'm honest as well …" he remained silent for a little while, becoming increasingly nervous. "This isn't the first time I've come here, you know. But since you spend your life locked away in your house …"

I sat next to him. "You've got something to tell me, but you don't know how to," I said to him.

He said nothing and watched the cars passing by. "Why don't we go for a bit of a walk before it starts to snow?" he suggested.

"Yes, why not."

We went down to the park, which was solitary and desolate in winter. The cold wind was rustling the dry leaves that remained on the ground. We walked slowly, our hands buried deep in our pockets.

"Well, there's someone who'd like to ask your forgiveness and send you his best wishes. In actual fact he'd like to send you a kiss."

"Who?"

"He gave me this for you."

He took a little package wrapped in gray paper out of his jacket pocket. The blood froze in my veins when I opened it. I turned pale. There, carefully folded, were José's blue Speedos.

"What's this?" I muttered, looking deep into his eyes.

"Take it easy, Javi, take it easy. Listen, don't take it like that. Don't start crying. It's all over, isn't it? Come on, calm down. We'll go and sit on that bench. Goddam, I knew it."

"Would you like to tell me what all this is about?" I said, standing and not making a move.

"Nothing, it's meant nicely, really. He can't see you—well, he doesn't want to see you, he thinks things are fine as they are, but …"

"Who? Who doesn't want to see me?"

"You know who. José Antonio, José. He felt very bad when he heard you were so ill, and he wants you to forgive him."

"So why doesn't he come and tell me this himself if he supposedly feels so bad about it?"

"No idea. I assume he's afraid of meeting you. But please don't take it like this, for goodness' sake."

We carried on walking. I suddenly felt weak again, and was

breathing with difficulty. The boy took my arm and we walked in silence for a while. Nevertheless, I noticed that the foul stench of all those dreadful memories was starting to dissipate, that it wasn't as strong anymore. A spark of life that had never completely died down was bringing color to my cheeks, caressed by the snowy breeze. I nervously lit a cigarette.

"Can I have one?"

It was at that moment, hearing that tone of voice, that I remembered. On the night when I'd met this blond guy and was going home at daybreak he'd thrown me a pack of cigarettes that didn't belong to me. I'd found my own pack a few minutes later up in my room. I smiled as I gave him a light.

"Keep the pack. It really belongs to you. That night, when you threw me a pack, I already had—"

"No," he interrupted, "it's yours."

"No, what I'm trying to explain to you is that I already had my pack of cigarettes. I'm sure you were getting confused."

"The pack I threw at you before I went—you'd left it on the diving board at the pool."

"What are you saying?"

"I saw you. You and José. I work at the pool in summer. I'm a friend of José, as you might have noticed by now. I was just finishing cleaning the kitchen at the cafeteria when you arrived that night. I saw you sitting on the diving board smoking, and I saw you go for a swim. Then you. And you left the cigarettes there."

I carried on walking in silence, taking short steps and linking arms with him. His words scratched at a scar rather than a memory, a scar that was still soft and tender, but a scar nevertheless and no longer a wound. I sighed.

"Then I followed you. Or to be more accurate I followed you on your own."

"Why did you follow me?"

153

"I don't really know …"

I looked at him gratefully. Of course he knew. We both knew.

"You took him home and then you came here to the park. I'm sure you can remember the rest yourself."

"Yes, of course I remember. And I also remember that you didn't tell me your name."

"My name is Miguel."

"I thought as much."

"Why?"

"José told me about a boy, a friend of his who works at the pool. That's his name."

He looked at me, nervous again, and took a long draw on his cigarette.

"What else did he tell you about me?"

I gave him a gentle smile. "That you're a really awesome guy."

"Is that all?"

"Well, as far as I can recall … that's all," I lied.

"Ah."

We stopped in front of the stone parapet by the river. I don't know if this was deliberate on his part or whether it was me who had cunningly brought us here: it was the precise spot where we had met many months ago.

"So you aren't really a prostitute?"

"Of course not."

"And all that talk, saying 'dude' every five seconds …?"

He went as red as a tomato. "That was to make you horny, and so I wouldn't give myself away."

"So you wouldn't give what away?"

"Oh, nothing. I didn't really mean it."

I laughed inside, yet at the same time was really touched by how nervous he was. "Oh yes, and how's your girlfriend, your 'chick'?"

"That was a lie too," he smiled, getting redder and redder, hiding his face and looking in the opposite direction to me.

We remained silent for a while. I turned around and stared at the sluggish gray water. "Why did you come here, Miguel?"

"To give you what José gave me."

"Was that the only reason?"

"Well, and to see how you were. I know you've been in hospital a couple of times. You were very ill, and the doctors are still keeping an eye on you but I can tell you're well, much better at least. But you need to eat a bit more, don't you? You're just skin and bones."

He laughed.

"And that was all you wanted?"

"Why else would I have come?" he asked softly.

"I don't know." I took his hand as I continued to look at the river. "Maybe to tell me you could have strangled me a hundred times that night, for example."

"A hundred isn't much," he smiled in embarrassment. "Doing what you did with me while all the time you were thinking about another guy …"

"Forgive me."

"No, there's nothing to forgive. I already knew. I only had to see how you looked at him. You were crazy about him. But that night I went home all by myself after I'd been with you, and ended up crying."

"I don't know if you remember the last kiss, the one I gave you just over there by the trees. I wasn't thinking about him. That kiss was for you."

"Of course I remember. And that's precisely why I hoped to see you again. Well, that's almost the only reason why I came today."

"Just because of that?"

"No, not just because of that. The truth is that, well, I wanted to know if you might be able to spare some time one of these days so

155

we could see each other again. Of course only if you want to, now that you're feeling better because you have to look after yourself, and I wouldn't like to …"

"Is tomorrow okay for you?" I looked at him. His blue eyes radiated sheer affection, the like of which I hadn't seen in a long time.

"Sure." His face lit up.

"Well, tomorrow then. Where shall we meet?"

"At your grandmother's house if you like, where the piano is."

"How do you know that?"

"I know much more about you than you might think," he whispered, and gently squeezed my hand.

He looked nervously to the left and right; there was no one in sight. Without further ado he closed his eyes and gave me a quick and furtive kiss on the lips.

"And that's why I came, too."

I smiled at him, wiped the rebellious hair from his forehead, linked arms with him and walked with him to the square. We said goodbye until the following day. I called out to him when he was already a little way off.

"Hey, Miguel!"

He turned around.

"You've forgotten your cigarettes!" I threw the pack toward him.

He picked it off the ground, laughed, waved his hand in the air and then ran off. The first tiny snowflakes were beginning to fall as I turned the corner of the avenue. It was at this very spot that José had kissed Beatriz in front of me on the day before we went to the Picos. I looked up into the sky from where the gentle snow was falling, then over to the rooftops. I could see smoke coming from chimneys, large picture windows, drab balconies, leafless trees, people hurrying to open their umbrellas, cars and traffic

156

lights, and the snow landing noiselessly and then disappearing on the dirty, checkered sidewalk. The eternal, ancient and yet ever-changing beauty of all this filled my heart. I suspected I was seeing it again for the first time in many years. I believed, knew in a way that's hard to explain that the world, my world had been waiting very patiently for the moment when I would look at it again with these eyes, the ones I'd always had. Everything that surrounded me had been waiting for a very long time, an infinity, to don its purest and most tranquil aspect, to embellish itself in readiness for the precise moment when I and I alone would return from that far-off place where I had gone astray. It had been waiting for me to reopen the rusty windows of my heart so I could lean out and contemplate everything afresh. Life carried on as it always had done, I was alive again, and my soul was cleansed and caressed by the return of this sweet, chilly air.

As I turned the corner by the cathedral, already close to my grandmother's house, my head was filled with a melody I had never heard, at first like a vague murmuring and then with utter clarity. It was a fast, high-pitched melody, rather like birds twittering in the sky and then swooping down, playful and exuberant, only to rise again time after time, sparkling like crystal, like a child's innocent laughter. I quickened my pace. I threw the package with the blue Speedos into a trash can as I tried to retain, to lock within my memory those sweet, smiling, optimistic notes. How lovely they would sound when I sat down at the piano.